First published in the UK by Beacon Books and Media Ltd
Earl Business Centre, Dowry Street, Oldham, OL8 2PF, UK.
Copyright © Akmal Ullah 2022

www.beaconbooks.net

Cataloging-in-Publication record for this book is available from the
British Library

ISBN 978-1-912356-48-5   Paperback
ISBN 978-1-912356-49-2   Ebook

Cover design by Moimoi.

THE COOKIE DEALER

Akmal Ullah

BEACON BOOKS

Acknowledgements

All thanks and praises are due onto Allah, who continues to shower me with His grace, bounty and blessings every day.

I want to thank my late father (may Allah have mercy on him) for showing with his actions the importance of having patience and gratitude in a world that can sometimes seem so dark and unfair; my mother for her constant daily prayers for my wellbeing; my wife Rayhana for her love, care and encouragement; my two children Yusra and Yunus who always brighten up my day no matter what has happened; my colleagues Lilith Johnstone, Rachael Burton and James Mansfield who very kindly provided me with critical feedback which helped develop and shape the story; my editor Siema Rafiq, for the endless times she examined the manuscript in order to help me improve, refine and enhance every aspect of the story and bring it to publishing standard; and finally a huge thank you to Jamil Chishti at Beacon Books for once again encouraging me to share my crazy creative ideas with the world.

Chapter 1

Shattering News

It was an unusually warm October afternoon on the last day of the autumn half-term break. Mum finally gave in to Aakil and Aahan's continuous chants of "ice cream in a cup, ice cream in a cup." They chanted in unison, rocking back and forth like they were in some sort of prayer.

"Just give it to them, Mum," I told her, rubbing my temples, "they're starting to give me a headache."

"I know, darling, I'll cross over the road and get two McFlurry ice creams. Do you want anything?" she asked, searching through her tattered small black handbag. I shook my head. "Stay here and keep an eye on your brothers, then we'll go and sit in the park for a bit."

We walked through the open rusty gates of the park and sat on a bench, trying to soak up some of the faint rays of sunshine that were slowly disappearing.

"Did you manage to revise everything over the holidays, Riya?" she asked, staring at me with her big hazel eyes as the wind threw her light brown hair across her face.

"Of course," I lied, trying to sound convincing. I looked away so she couldn't read my face.

"Good stuff," she added, "you're only a few months away from your final A-Level exams, Riya, and I want you to be well-prepared so you can reach your full potential." Her voice was serious and monotone.

"Can we please stop talking about it, Mum?" I pleaded, rolling my eyes. "Let me forget about studying, just for this afternoon."

"Did you just roll your eyes at me?" she asked, smiling. "Alright, I'll stop talking about exams—for now—but you should really let me put some mascara on those beautiful eyes." Mum let out a sigh and looked closely at me.

"No, Mum, stop it, you know I don't like fussing with make-up." I placed my right hand on top of Mum's hand as her phone started to vibrate inside her handbag.

Mum took out her phone and looked at it, blinking several times as she brought it closer to her face. Her lips began to tremble. She turned towards me and stared blankly.

"I know that number," she mumbled, taking rapid, short breaths. She began gasping for air.

"What is it, Mum? Who is it?"

"It's them, Riya, it's the hospital." Mum swallowed hard and looked at me. She took a deep breath before accepting the call. "Hello," she answered, trying to stop her voice from cracking. Mum hated the way her voice became squeaky when she was tense, so she tried not to speak much. But the fear and panic in her voice was unmistakable.

I heard the voice at the other end of the call very clearly. "Mrs Kaur, the results have arrived. I'm sorry, but I'm afraid it's bad news—the biopsies came back showing that the cancer has returned and is now much more advanced than the last time. Your cancer is now metastatic—meaning it's secondary cancer that has spread to other parts of the body. We're going to need you to come in as soon as possible."

We looked at each other, trembling as Mum put the phone down. I shot a look at Aakil and Aahan, who were playing on the swings and laughing. They looked so innocent, so carefree. Whereas my world had just come crashing down.

The short walk home from Crescent Park was eerily silent. I kept quiet. I didn't know what to say. Mum pressed her lips together, trying to hold back the tears, but it didn't work; small droplets slowly trickled out one at a time and fell down her cheeks. She looked away and wiped her eyes and nose with a tissue, smudging her carefully applied mascara and eyeliner each time. She ran her fingers through her hair and exhaled heavily.

I had a giant lump in my throat that made me feel like I couldn't swallow. I tried to hold myself together, at least for the sake of my brothers—I didn't want them to realise what was happening.

I followed on behind Mum as she slowly walked home holding Aakil and Aahan's hands, one on each side. They continued to jump, hop and poke each other as they always did, oblivious to what was going on.

It was only our second week in our new flat on the Bridge Tower inside the Southern Estate—the council placed us there temporarily until they could find us somewhere permanent; a process that was taking forever even though Dad was bidding for homes every week on

3

their website. Our flat on the Bridge Tower had lots of problems; it was cold, draughty and the bedrooms had a strong damp smell, but it was home for now. Other residents complained about mice and rats that you could see scurrying around the bin area, but the council never did anything about it.

I reached for the giant communal door. It was badly damaged and hanging on one hinge. I carefully opened it to let Mum and the boys in, hoping that it wouldn't collapse on us. At first, my mind went completely blank as we plodded up the plain concrete stairs and into our flat. My footsteps felt slow and heavy as I dragged myself up to the second floor. As soon as we all got in, I ran to my bedroom and firmly shut the door behind me. My stomach churned, my legs became wobbly and my mind started firing horrible images faster than a machine gun. I kept visualising Mum's pale face shrouded in white inside an open casket. I closed my eyes for a few seconds, and when I opened them again, everything felt blurry. I stood up quickly to bring myself back to normality, but I couldn't stand. My knees buckled and I fell to the floor like a crumpled piece of paper. I couldn't help it. A faint whimper forced itself out of my mouth. *I can't do this, not again!*

I wanted it to all go away; the confusion, the emptiness, the fear. I didn't want to speak to anyone, not even Anisa, who was my best friend, but I knew bottling everything up inside wasn't a good idea. I needed to get some of these horrible feelings off my chest, so I quickly typed a text message to Anisa explaining everything and pressed send before turning my phone off. I closed my eyes, trying to shut everything out.

I woke up early the next morning, even before my alarm clock went off. My sleep was broken throughout the whole night. Every time I dozed off, I suddenly woke up with my heart beating fast. I kept seeing Mum in my dreams every time I closed my eyes, so I gave up trying to force myself to sleep and instead lay in bed with my blanket up to my face for most of the night.

I peeped through the door to see Mum and Dad sitting by the small kitchen table. I looked at Dad's face; his eyes were red and swollen. He quickly wiped his eyes and turned away as he saw me. His slim figure looked even smaller as he leaned forward and stared mindlessly at the floor.

"I'll call them now to make an appointment, love," he said as he got up, clearing his throat, "let's see what they say."

"What if I need surgery again... how are we gonna...?" Mum inhaled and rubbed her temples. "You know the NHS won't cover everything—they didn't the last time."

"I know," he replied, exhaling deeply.

"How will we cope when we're still relying on food banks for...?" She took a deep breath and sighed, without finishing her sentence.

"I know, I'll find a way," he replied, crouching down to hold Mum. Dad kissed her on the forehead and walked out of the kitchen.

I felt a stab of guilt listening to their conversation—I wished I could do something to help Dad with the finances.

I wanted to get a part-time job during my A-Levels but Mum and Dad told me to focus solely on my studies; they didn't want me to get distracted.

"Let me know when it is, Mum, I want to come too," I said, popping my head in.

"Of course, darling," she replied, wiping her tears, "let me get the boys ready for school."

I took a few sips of my tea and set off. Despite everything that was happening, it was an important day. Being part of the Prefect Team at my Sixth Form college came with responsibilities. I had to take a deep breath, get to college and pretend everything was normal.

Chapter 2

School Politics

I felt the breeze on my face as I rushed to get to school in time for the meeting. I watched the leaves slowly shake off the branches before gliding like a bird as they hit the ground and roamed the floors beneath. I tried to keep calm as I walked over the drying green and pale brown leaves, which crunched under my feet.

I saw Anisa in the distance. Wearing a dark maroon-coloured headscarf against her long black skirt and loose jumper, she stood up straight, her eyes searching for me. She always looked so confident and elegant. I tried not to get upset as I approached Anisa at the end of my road, but it didn't work. She peered at me with her big watery light brown eyes without saying anything. For a few seconds, I stood there looking at her face—her flawless skin glowed and her silver nose ring sparkled. I don't know why, but her familiar face brought out a new silent storm that had been brewing inside my chest. As she grabbed me and held me tightly against her, I couldn't help it; I sobbed on her shoulder uncontrollably.

"Babe, it'll be ok *inshallah*, you'll see." Anisa smiled at me and wiped away my tears. "Now come on, find the strength to carry on like you did the last time!"

"Annie, what am I going to do if she... you know?" I swallowed hard; I didn't want to say the word. "How will we cope without her?"

Anisa grabbed me by the shoulders and stared hard into my eyes. "She's gonna be OK, you hear? Take her to the hospital, let them start her treatment again and hold on to the hope that she'll get through it again."

"I wish I could be as strong as Mum needs me to be, but I'm not, sometimes I feel like I'm crumbling." I wiped my nose again and dabbed my eyes.

Anisa gawked at me incredulously. "Crumbling? The clever, witty, intelligent Riya I know will never crumble, alright?! Now get back on the horse and let's hope we can get you to school on time to save little Harith. I would have stepped in for you, but I don't even know what happened."

"It's fine," I told her, "I guess that's what we signed up for when we got voted into the Prefect Team. Duty calls!"

Harith sat very still outside the Principal's office as if the chair was sucking him in.

"Try to relax," I told him, trying to force a smile on my rigid face.

"I'm trying," he whimpered, gritting his teeth. "It's just, I've never been in trouble before—not like this anyway." He wiped his forehead and put his hands on his cheeks. "I wonder what they're gonna do to me?"

As part of the Sixth Form Prefect Team, I was there to support him. We waited for his dad to arrive and accompany us to a meeting with our Head of Sixth Form, Mr Gorton, which was going to take place in the Meeting Room beside the Principal's office. "You know I didn't start it, right? I was defending myself—I wasn't going to let myself get bullied by that thug!" he frowned.

"It doesn't make it right though, does it? I'll try to convince them to go easy on you," I whispered, handing him my cup of water—he looked like he needed it more than I did.

Harith was in trouble for attacking Syed, or the "Tooth Fairy" as he liked to be called, which I found hard to believe since Syed was physically bigger, taller and broader than Harith. Syed always walked around with his chest thrust out which made him look like a brick wall. Nobody messed with him.

"I swear to God, he attacked me first after I refused to hand over more of my profits and sell his stuff..." he stopped short of finishing his sentence, clenched his fists and let out a deep sigh. "I wasn't gonna do it... sell his stuff I mean, that's not what I'm about!"

Break and lunch times were when the school turned into a marketplace for student entrepreneurs—something that our new Principal, Mr Faulkner, encouraged, especially after our school became an enterprise academy last year. At break times, students advertised what stock they had and lunch times were when money and goods exchanged hands.

"What are you talking about?" I asked. "Why was Syed trying to take your profits and what did he try to force you to sell?"

"It doesn't matter anymore. Anyway, I'm not a snitch!"

"Regardless of what he did to provoke you, Harith," I said, "Mr Phillips, the Business and Economics teacher, wrote a Referral saying he saw you attack Syed. You can't go around having a scuffle with everyone who annoys you." I looked at my watch, hoping to get the meeting over with.

"Mr Phillips?" he scoffed, "Mr Phillips didn't even see the fight!"

"OK, well I'll try to challenge it then," I reassured him.

"Why am I the only one here?" he growled. "Syed should be here—he started the whole thing, he's been irritating me for weeks!"

"I can bring that all up when Mr Gorton calls us in," I explained, "but you're going to have to tell me a little bit more."

"There's no point," he sighed, shaking his head. "It will only make things worse and no one will believe me anyway!"

The school allowed Sixth Formers to sell anything they could get their hands on, but food always sold really well, which I'm sure the school canteen wasn't too happy about! We all knew how it worked—groups of Sixth Formers organised themselves into teams and bought cookies, crisps and doughnuts from supermarkets when prices were reduced on stock that was coming close to its sell-by date, which they then sold in different parts of the school. There was always a real buzz during break and lunch times.

As Harith's father arrived, we were told to go to the Meeting Room where Mr Gorton and Mr Phillips were waiting, sat at one end of the oval-shaped table. I took a chair and sat at the table, while Harith and his father were asked to sit on the other side.

"Mr Phillips will be with us this morning," he revealed, clearing his throat, "as an observer."

Harith and I looked at each other but didn't say anything. It's not like we could object anyway.

Mr Gorton had a huge bundle of papers in his hand—probably Harith's most recent assessment results, and his attendance and punctuality reports, which he placed on the table. Mr Phillips took a seat next to him and tried to make himself look useful by shuffling through the bundle of papers.

This was the first time in his entire time at school that Harith was in trouble. He was normally a good student: he was well-behaved, and his assessment grades, attendance and punctuality were also fine.

Harith couldn't sit still; he was very fidgety, biting his fingernails and his bottom lip. He was probably afraid that this incident would affect any reference that Mr Gorton wrote for him when he made applications to go to university.

"Harith attacked a student in the presence of a member of staff," began Mr Gorton.

"I saw the whole thing, I was there," interrupted Mr Phillips. Mr Gorton gave him a peculiar look.

"OK, Mr Phillips," he said abruptly, turning his head towards Mr Phillips and holding out his hand. "If you'll allow me to continue."

Mr Phillips opened his mouth as if to say something, but decided against it. My eyes flitted between the two teachers. Something didn't seem right, but I couldn't put my finger on it.

He then faced us again. "This school is where learning takes place and we do not tolerate this kind of behaviour," he added, sifting through a bunch of papers, probably to try and find something to prove his point—that's what usually happened in these situations! But he couldn't find anything and soon gave up.

"I'm sorry about what I did, Sir," Harith murmured, gritting his teeth.

His father made no attempt to excuse or defend his son's actions. He knew what his son had done was wrong. "Mr Gorton," he said apologetically. "I'm very sorry my son behaved like this. I've already had strong words with him at home and I assure you he won't do anything like this again."

Harith leaned sideways and whispered into my ear. "Dad knows exactly what happened."

"Shhhh, stay focused, let's just get through this first!"

I stepped in to try to support Harith. Acting like his defence lawyer in a courtroom, I did my best to persuade Mr Gorton to give out the lightest sanction possible by reading out a statement I typed up over the weekend.

"Mr Gorton Sir, Harith is very sorry for his behaviour. He has an exemplary record in this school in terms of his behaviour, learning and relationships with staff and pupils. He is deeply disappointed in his conduct and is very remorseful. That's why I would humbly ask you to accept his apology without giving him a formal sanction and let Harith put this whole episode behind him."

Mr Phillips sat there taking notes. I was sure I heard him snigger.

But Mr Gorton didn't notice him and as I expected, he didn't listen to me either. He already had a sanction planned for Harith, which wasn't too bad, to be honest. As the short meeting ended, he declared that Harith was banned from selling anything on the school premises and would be placed on a Behaviour Monitoring Report until the end of this new half-term. The report had to be signed and monitored by the teachers who were on break and lunch supervision duties and Harith had to report to the Principal at the end of every day. Failing to meet any of his targets would mean an immediate internal exclusion followed by a final warning.

"This isn't the end," he whispered into my ear. "I'm not scared of Syed. I'll have to find a way to carry on selling my stuff without running into him!"

Harith quietly left the meeting to go to his next lesson, appearing to show remorse, but acknowledging a secret wink from his father.

I came out of the meeting feeling deflated. *What was the point of me supporting Harith in there if Mr Gorton wasn't even going to listen to a single thing I said?* I was beginning to think being in the Prefect Team was a complete waste of time. I was lost in this train of thought when Nadim walked in through the Reception area. He stopped by the long mirror in front of the sliding doors and looked at himself as he ran his fingers through his thick black hair. He was wearing black chino trousers, a light cream coloured jumper, a navy blazer and grey loafer type shoes. I looked past him, pretending that I didn't notice him, but he looked straight back at me.

"Riya!" he called out as he slowly walked towards me. My heart started to thump against my rib cage like a hammer as he got closer. I tried not to stare at those sparkly eyes, but I couldn't help it; they were hypnotizing. He had a small goatee—I assumed to make that baby face of his look a bit older. It didn't work; he still looked like he belonged in an up-and-coming boy band. I sensed the blushing coming on, so I quickly looked down at the floor —anywhere except his face.

"Still doing the Prefect thing then?" His smile gave rise to an irresistible dimple that warmed up my insides. I found the courage to look back up at his dark cat-like eyes. I bet he was trying to keep me blushing—he was definitely doing a good job!

"Yeah," I replied casually, trying desperately not to stumble over my words. "It will look good on my university application, I'm sure."

"Typical Riya," he laughed, "always planning meticulously for the future. I don't even know what I'm doing tomorrow. I just take each day as it comes."

"Well some of us need to plan, otherwise things don't work out like they obviously do in your life." My mouth slowly formed into a smile; it was beyond my control. I don't know why I felt like that every time I saw Nadim. We'd known each other since primary school, but I'd never really spoken to him beyond that even though I really wanted to. We'd just occasionally bump into each other and say hello.

"It's good though, what you're doing I mean," he continued, "I heard about what happened with Harith and Syed. I hope you managed to get Mr Gorton to go easy on him."

"He didn't listen," I replied, "I shouldn't have wasted my time."

"Well, I'm sure Harith appreciated it."

"I hope so. Harith said a few things that didn't make sense—I'm sure there was more to what happened than I know," I said, my eyes gazing at the floor beneath us, lost in thought.

"What do you mean?" he asked.

Just then I spotted Anisa in the background coming towards us. "Riya!" she called.

Nadim took this as a cue to leave. "Anyway, I've gotta go, Riya, see you later." He smiled and I watched him drift into the crowd as the pips sounded to indicate it was time for the first lesson.

"That was Nadim, right?" Anisa giggled.

"What are you laughing about?" I asked.

"Nothing. You should have seen the way you were looking at him." She gave me a peculiar look.

"Oh my God, shut up, Anisa," I said, trying to sound annoyed. "I didn't look at him in any way."

"He is cute though," she continued. A wisp of jealousy made my stomach clench. I didn't reply. "Be careful yeah, he's a good Muslim boy—that means he doesn't date."

"Why are you even going there?"

"Just saying."

As we walked to lesson, I noticed a boy being wheeled into the medical room behind the Reception area in the school's makeshift wheelchair.

"What's happened there?" I asked Anisa.

"Some of these boys have started vaping—who knows what they put in those things. He must have had a reaction after smoking it!"

"Seriously? How are they getting hold of that stuff in school?"

"God knows who's bringing it in, but the situation is out of control—these kids probably get it from the older lot in Sixth Form. The school will have to call the ambulance. They don't know how to deal with someone who's had a reaction to vaping that rubbish."

My mind raced back to some of the things Harith said about Syed—I didn't know what he meant, but I was sure I didn't have the whole picture.

Chapter 3

Mum's Battle

Mum was first diagnosed with breast cancer only two years ago and went through chemotherapy and radiography, before having surgery earlier this year, which Dad had to pay for. Luckily she made a full recovery. But our happiness was short-lived; now, two weeks into our move to the Bridge Tower, Mum's cancer had come back. Cuts to the NHS meant that Dad paid for the previous surgery by taking out bank loans and maxing out his credit cards. They both tried to hide that sort of stuff from me, but I knew he was in debt and paying it off bit by bit.

How would we manage this time if Dad had to pay for Mum's treatment again? We could barely manage without going to the local food bank and taking things from the free community section of Mr Cooper's mini-market across the road. My mind always spiralled out of control when I worried so much; I couldn't stop the trail of negative thoughts, like I was falling into a bottomless rabbit hole.

I couldn't believe that the stability we had been craving for such a long time hadn't lasted. As a family, we finally felt a little settled: we were starting to get used to the new flat, Dad started his new job as a prison officer, Mum seemed much healthier, and Aakil and Aahan adjusted into their new primary schools. I was in the final year of my A-Levels at a Sixth Form college not too far from home so there was no need to change schools. The only thing I had left to worry about was finishing my A-Levels and getting into a good university. But that dreadful phone call changed everything.

I didn't know if Mum could fight it again. My mind kept telling me that very soon, we would have to say goodbye to her. How would Dad and the little ones cope if Mum passed away? What would I do? I didn't know and I didn't want to think like that, but my mind kept shooting these questions at me like arrows.

I wasn't ready to let go. I frantically searched the internet about her condition and possible treatments. I went on some forums where people were speaking about their experiences with cancer treatment. I went on the Bellington Hospital website—the private hospital where she had her previous surgery. It wasn't cheap! I thought long and hard about how I could possibly make money to help pay for any treatment we could get for Mum.

I had to wait until Mum's hospital appointment came around, but until then I needed to find something to keep myself busy and distract myself. Cooking was the only thing that helped, baking in particular. I loved to bake things: cakes, brownies and chocolate cookies. I always watched cooking programmes on TV: *Come Dine With Me, The Hairy Bikers, The Great British Bake Off* and *Master Chef.* I couldn't cook as well as some of them on those programmes, but I did know how to bake a good cake and make some yummy cookies.

Cookies—that was my distraction for now. In the early part of the evening, I decided to make some for everyone. I started by heating our oven to 375ºF. I then mixed sugar, butter, vanilla and egg into a large bowl and stirred in flour, baking soda, salt and chocolate chips. Finally, I dropped the dough in rounded tablespoonfuls about two inches apart onto a greased cookie sheet and baked for about twenty minutes until the cookies became light brown around the edges but still soft in the centre.

When they came out of the oven, the entire kitchen was filled with a strong warm sugar scent. You could almost taste the vanilla extract and the semi-sweet chocolate in the air. The light brown cookies brightened up the kitchen like little circles of sunlight.

"Be careful, Riya, use the oven gloves to take them out please!" Mum looked at me and smiled. "You obviously know what cheers me up! I just need to brew some *chai* now."

Mum was flipping *paratha* flatbreads on the pan whilst simultaneously taking bites of her cookie and sipping her tea when Anisa came over. She flung open the kitchen window, which made the sounds from outside drift in. The strong stench of cigarette smoke and other odours slowly crept in through the small gap; there were always youngsters smoking on our block.

"Hi, Aunty! Cookies? Yummy! I could have a whole jar of Riya's cookies and I wouldn't even feel guilty," Anisa laughed, taking huge bites.

"Guilty? You hardly need to watch your weight, Annie."

"Yeah, thank you and don't forget to say *mashallah* before you accidentally give me the evil eye," she said, reaching for a cookie.

"Say what?" I asked.

"Never mind, anyway, you're the opposite; you could do with some weight, my little cookie hustler. I know you're not that gawky-eyed girl with braces anymore, but you're still so thin!"

"Cookie hustler?" I frowned, smiling. "You make me sound so shifty! Anyway, I'm actually not that thin. You're not jealous, are you Annie?" I joked.

"Jealous? Well, maybe a little," she laughed. "Who isn't jealous of your natural beauty? You don't even need to take time applying make-up like I do."

"Stop it, Annie."

"Do you girls want some *parathas* or *samosas*?" asked Mum. We both shook our heads and went upstairs to my bedroom, her eyes following us as we left.

It's a good thing Dad was at work—I don't know why, but he always eyed me with suspicion every time Anisa came over. He never said anything horrible to Anisa or acted weird in front of her, but it was just a feeling I got every time I spoke about hanging around with her. Maybe it was because Anisa was a Muslim girl—he probably preferred me to be closer to some of my other friends like our neighbour Preeti, but to me it didn't make a difference. Mum always taught me to respect everyone no matter what they believed or what colour they were. I made friends with whoever I clicked with.

We were a Hindu family; my parents were from Gujarat, but we weren't really religious at all. When I was a lot younger, we marked religious festivals at school like Eid, Diwali, Christmas and Easter, which was really fun. Everyone would bring in food, drinks and sweets and we would all get together and have a bit of a party. As I grew older,

20

I paid less attention to religion, even though questions about belief would sometimes bug me.

Sitting on one side of my single bed, I felt stifled tears welling up in my eyes. I pressed my lips together, inhaled and exhaled—I didn't want to get emotional in front of Anisa again.

Anisa put her phone down, untied her *hijab*, letting her glossy curly black hair with blonde highlights flow out and bounce on her shoulders.

"Wow, gorgeous," I marvelled, "when did you dye your hair?"

"Oh, just last week," she replied, "I never stay one colour for too long!"

"If you take so much care to maintain such beautiful hair, why do you hide it in a *hijab*?" I asked, trying not to sound too personal.

"A *hijab* doesn't mean you're having a bad hair day every day you know," she said sarcastically. "I can still have lovely hair. But my *deen*, Islam, tells me to cover my hair."

"What does that mean?" I asked.

"*Deen* means a way of life, my darling," she replied, taking my hairbrush out of my drawer. "It's not just some rituals you do in a mosque or at home," she continued. "It's a complete way of life; from what you eat, to the way you dress, treat others and your relationship with God."

"I do admire your devotion," I said, "I guess religion can bring a lot of peace in a person's life. That's why you wear full sleeve stuff even on hot days, right?"

"Yep," she replied casually, before turning around to look at me intensely. She was wearing eyeliner, which made her wide brown eyes look even bigger. I was always a little jealous of how she was able to perfectly deploy the arsenal of make-up in her bag the way a superhero uses their powers. It made her skin look so flawless.

"I came to see if you were alright," she said, "you texted to tell me that the appointment is tomorrow. It'll be ok, I'm praying for you."

I felt a huge lump in my throat as my eyes started watering. My eyes burned as I blinked rapidly. I wanted to turn away before I burst out into huge heaving sobs, but I couldn't help myself.

"I'm terrified, Annie," I whispered in a flurry of tears, "I'm so scared that we might lose her."

Anisa grabbed me and pulled me towards her. I rested my head on her left shoulder so she couldn't see my ugly sobs.

"It'll be ok, babe," she said, "you have to have faith and hope for the best."

"Faith? I don't know how to have faith," I said, wiping my tears on my right sleeve.

"You have to raise your hands and pray to God. He answers everyone," she said, smiling.

"Which one? Which God should I pray to?" I asked, desperate for an answer.

"We believe that there is only one God—Allah, the Most Gracious, the Most Merciful," she explained.

"Why would He listen to me?" I took out a tissue from the packet on my bedside table and wiped my eyes and nose, trying to make sense of what Anisa was saying.

"He listens to everyone. Just call upon Him and no one else, and I promise He will answer."

I swallowed hard and nodded.

Anisa stood up and then bent over to rub my shoulders before gripping my arms.

"It'll be alright," she said commandingly, "your Mum will be fine. Let them see her, work out a treatment plan and you stay strong! Don't forget to say a few prayers before you sleep. Leave it to Allah and trust Him, in the end, all will be well, you'll see." She winked and smiled at me before tucking her hair away in one swoop of a scarf and a strategically placed silver safety pin. "I've gotta go, let me know what happens tomorrow."

After Anisa left, I was completely lost in worry again; I couldn't help it. I paced up and down my bedroom trying to think of a way out of this problem. I walked sometimes with my hands behind my back, and at other times running my fingers through my hair, stroking my temples and cheeks. Sometimes I squeezed my temples so my brain would just stop thinking, but it was no use. It was no good—this wasn't normal. I was supposed to be a very intelligent girl—I achieved some of the highest GCSE grades in my year group almost two years ago. I was performing very well, I was set to achieve very high grades at A-Level and I was part of the Prefect Team at school. But all that maturity and intelligence seemed to have become temporarily blocked as I battled with my mind, trying to stop it from worrying. Then I remembered what Anisa told me: "Pray!"

I didn't know how to, but my head automatically looked up towards the sky and for the first time, I made my palms into a cup shape and raised my hands in prayer. I took a deep breath and said whatever came to my mind.

"I know there is someone out there and I'm sure you can hear me," I cried, "please don't let Mum die, not now! She only just recovered. Please God, I know I've never turned to you before, but this time I really could do with some help. Please help my Mum, don't let her die, we need her, I'm sure you know that. And please, please, help me stay strong and get a grip of my emotions. Don't let me crack!"

After I finished, I felt a little lighter. I threw myself onto my bed and under my blanket, scrunching myself into a ball. As I tucked myself in, I faintly heard Mum and Dad talking in the kitchen whilst washing up the dishes and the boys were whispering about something in their bedroom. My room wasn't cold, but I shivered, even under the covers. Sleep was pulling at me, so I gave in and closed my eyes...

It was a warm summer's morning. I was wearing a light grey shawl that complemented my loose fluttering beige gown. I walked forward, gradually taking in the sunlight, inhaling the fresh air and feeling bits of the long grass graze against the sides of my feet. A small section of Crescent Park appeared to be cordoned off like when the art exhibitions took place there in early August every year. I looked straight, then left and then right. I felt the presence of lots of people but I couldn't see anyone. Again I looked left, right and straight ahead, adjusting my vision each time due to the sunlight, but nothing seemed out of the ordinary. Finally, I turned around to look behind and there it was—a huge banner, which read "Riya's Tasty Treats". With a sudden sense of excitement, I looked everywhere to find the entrance. As I came closer to the banner, I heard the voices of people talking, which was getter louder and louder, but again, I couldn't trace the source of the voices. I looked carefully in every direction again as far as my vision allowed. I could see perfectly well, but I still couldn't find the source of the loud chatter that was now beginning to annoy me. I began to feel restless and almost gave up. Just then, in the corner of my eye, I saw some faint lights on the ground. As I approached it, I saw other lights—they were spotlights on the ground carving a pathway to a black door, which had a golden door knob and some symmetrical patterns at the top. It was slightly ajar.

I walked in. There were loads of people inside, but nobody noticed me. Bright lights dazzled my eyes and made the room feel even stuffier. I passed by a lot of people and walked straight ahead to what looked like a stage. Before climbing the stairs onto the stage, to my left I saw what looked like boxes and boxes of the same item; I couldn't make out what it was. It looked like packets of biscuits wrapped in shiny blue and purple wrapping paper—airtight so you couldn't smell anything. I slowly climbed the stairs and walked onto the stage. I approached what was the podium, which had a laptop and several typed notes next to it entitled "My Presentation by Riya Kaur". The laptop screen was on standby. I clicked one of the buttons, making the presentation page appear on the massive screen behind me. Suddenly, everyone noticed me. For a few seconds, they just stared at me.

"It's her," said one voice. "That's Riya!" Loud cheers followed and everyone stood up from their seats clapping. I stood there in utter shock and amazement.

I opened my eyes suddenly as the sunlight streamed through my curtains. "What was that?" I uttered under my breath. *It was such a weird dream—it was probably all the stress and worry sending confusing messages to my brain. Or maybe it meant something?* I thought to myself.

Chapter 4

The Sting in my Ears

I went with Mum and Dad to the hospital appointment that weekend. I was already awake by the time I heard Dad's rushed footsteps early that morning as he paced around, bumping into almost everything.

"Are you alright, Dad?" I asked, staring at his blank face. His eyes wandered searchingly. He ran back and forth from his bedroom and the bathroom with his bathrobe half-tied and a toothbrush in one hand—he clearly wasn't good at multi-tasking.

"I'm alright, love," he finally answered, drying his slowly thinning hair with a brown towel. "You couldn't be a darling and make me some coffee, could you? I overslept a little. I was up late bidding for homes—hopefully we'll get something soon!"

"I've already made it for you, Dad, it's on the kitchen table with your toast." I finished ironing his shirt and trousers and handed them to him.

"Thanks, Riya," he smiled, chewing on his toast. "I couldn't get the whole day off work, so I'll have to go in after the appointment."

I looked at his face—he looked tired, worn out. I knew shift work was difficult for Dad, but he never complained.

"Why don't you just take the day off today, Dad?"

"If only it was that easy," he mumbled, "I'm still on my probation period for the next three months. Your

27

Mum was restless last night—we both were, to be honest," he said, fixing his tie and pulling his jumper over his shoulders.

"You must be tired."

"It doesn't matter, you get ready and then wake your mum." Dad sipped his coffee again and started to get Mum's medical documents together along with her medications. I sat next to him and watched him finish off his breakfast in a rush. I wanted to tell him how I was feeling; the worry about Mum, how I wished I could help, but he must have had a lot on his mind too so I didn't want to offload on him.

By the time I finished my breakfast and got ready, Mum was up and dressed.

"Let's go," she said. Mum took long breaths and pressed her lips against each other. "I don't want to be late. I've dropped off the boys next door for a few hours."

"Mum, I made you tea and I've lightly buttered your toast, just the way you like it," I said, hoping she would eat something.

"Thanks, darling," she replied, taking a small sip of her tea and staring at her piece of toast, "but I'm not that hungry, to be honest."

The Mint Wing of St Christopher's Hospital was the oldest part of the hospital building. The entrance had lots of pictures of the hospital rugby team from the 1950s, which was placed on the plain white coloured entrance wall. The wooden floors looked clean but worn out with large gaps in between the floorboards; gaps that gathered dirt and turned into thick, black lines. The high ceilings of the long wide corridors created a sense of a never-ending pathway that would eventually lead to a dead-end or a ditch somewhere. The weekends were supposed to be the busiest, but the Mint Wing was really silent and still. The floors had probably been mopped recently—I saw a yellow "beware of the slippery floor" sign as we walked in and the strong smell of disinfectant overpowered the smell of freshly cut flowers from the Friends of St Christopher's flower shop by the entrance.

When we tried to check Mum in, the woman at the reception couldn't find her records.

"How could this be? She's been in and out of hospitals for the past two years, she was only here a couple of weeks ago!" Dad snapped. He sighed heavily. I could see he was trying not to get frustrated.

"I'm really sorry," said the lady hesitantly. "I just can't seem to... hold on... nope, I still can't find her. Are you sure it was this hospital you came to?"

A slow temper was working its way through my body—it was about to burst out like a can of fizzy drink that had been shaken too much. How could they not find her records? Before Mum could say something, I snapped at the receptionist.

"What on earth is going on here?" I said, "This is just ridiculous! How can you not find her records? What's happened to them?" I gritted my teeth. "How do they just magically disappear?"

"Wait a second... oh wait, there we are. I've found them. I'm really sorry about this, it's the IT system here, it's very slow and unreliable—it hasn't been updated for the last ten years. The system often loses people's data. We sometimes have to wait hours for someone from the IT team to come and search the backup drives, but you're lucky, we've managed to locate them! I've booked you in. Go straight through and take a seat in the waiting area. I'm sorry about the confusion," she said in a soft apologetic voice as she forced a smile.

I held Mum's hand as we walked into the waiting area. The light blue coloured chairs looked more exhausted than us. There was a strange shadowy shape on the seat I headed towards—probably proof that the chair had served patients very well.

Mum appeared frighteningly detached from all of it—emotionless even. At times my worries made me think I was the ill one. Mum didn't show any signs of worry, she just sat there in the waiting area, not really smiling, but not really showing any signs of sadness either. I realised that Mum must have come to terms with what was happening to her; she had come to accept it, I think. She cried when the doctors first told her, but not anymore, and definitely not in front of us.

Dad couldn't sit still; he kept breathing heavily and looked around mindlessly. I watched as he bit his lower lip and his nostrils became enlarged as he sniffed, trying to hold back his emotions.

The place was full of different kinds of people—young, old, black, white, Asian. In front of us, I saw a young couple with three children—one of which was still in a baby buggy. The couple sat side by side holding hands with one child each on their laps. The mother used her other hand to occasionally push the pram backwards and forwards each time the baby fidgeted. She looked as if she just woke up and came straight to the hospital. She definitely wasn't wearing any make-up, her hair was tied back with a plastic hair band and her clothes were pretty simple looking too; a pair of denim jeans, brown boots, a grey top, a black cardigan and a stripy scarf around her neck—a huge mismatch. The father sat still with his head facing down.

I looked around to see if I could read anyone else's face. No one was smiling. They all looked very tense and worried: some had huge bags under their eyes like they weren't sleeping very well, others couldn't stop fidgeting. One man was constantly walking up and down the corridor by the waiting area, and I saw one couple crying as they both came out of the consultant's room. *They must have had some really bad news.*

Thankfully, we didn't have to wait for too long. We arrived at our appointment on time and the clinic didn't seem too busy. The time people spent in the consultant's room couldn't have been more than five or ten minutes at most.

They called us in.

"Hi... ah, Mrs Kaur isn't it? I'm Dr Alan and I'm here to advise you about your planned treatment and answer any questions you may have," he said in a lowered voice. He sounded as if he was talking with his chest and not his throat, like someone who was struggling to breathe or had just recovered from a bad cough. I don't know why he sounded like that, but it didn't make what he said next any easier to digest. His words were like a barrage of pellets in my ear.

"Mrs Kaur, I've looked at the results of your recent biopsies and your previous medical history." He began scanning through various documents from the brown folder on his desk. "I'm afraid, this time it really is different and again, the NHS can only provide a limited amount of care and treatment for you."

Dad swallowed hard. "What does that mean?" he asked.

"It means that we can start her on chemotherapy again once a month, but I'm afraid the cancer is much more advanced this time and therefore the likely chance of any success is very slim. We are also not able to offer any form of surgery on the NHS."

"What do you mean, doctor?" I said, "Mum's going to be ok, right? She is going to get better, right?"

He didn't answer me directly.

"I'm very sorry, there is nothing more we can do here. I wish we could. I can give you some tablets to ease the pain and it should help you rest at night when things get bad," he continued hesitantly, avoiding eye contact with us.

I knew what his cold and emotionless words meant. I guess that was his job and he was probably so used to giving people bad news that he became numb to it. *I bet he wouldn't have been numb if he was losing someone he loved.*

"I know, doctor, it's quite alright. I understand," was all Mum said, trying to maintain her composure. I could see she was having a difficult time. Her lips trembled and she kept pushing them against each other. She rubbed her hands together, wiped her lips and put her hand over her mouth several times to hide her emotions.

"No," Dad interrupted, "surely there is something more you can do for her?! What's the point of chemotherapy if you think it's not gonna work?"

"We can only try," replied the doctor, closing Mum's medical file.

"This can't be right," Dad whimpered, "you mean we might lose her this time?" He let out a stifled cry.

"It's fine," whispered Mum, taking Dad's hand, "let's get out of here, I need to pick up the boys."

"If you see the Receptionist, she'll draw up a plan to start your chemotherapy within the next two weeks."

We got up to leave. Just as we started to walk towards the door, his voice made us turn around.

"There is another type of treatment, Mrs Kaur," said the doctor.

Mum and I looked at each other and then towards the doctor again.

"It's still in the early trial stages," he continued, "but I'm afraid it's not available on the NHS."

"What kind of treatment? Where can we get it?" I asked.

"The only treatment available to her at this late stage is immunotherapy, which is a treatment drug that works by using the immune system to destroy cancer cells. This treatment can be used on top of the chemotherapy sessions, and it would give you a slightly better chance of recovery, but again the chances of success at this stage are very low."

"Where is it available?" asked Dad.

"It's available at the Bellington Hospital, not too far from here, which is a private hospital as you know and so the treatment would need to be paid for privately."

I sensed that Mum didn't want to be there any longer, so I grabbed her hand and pulled her up.

"We'll look into it," said Dad, wiping his nose with his handkerchief.

We saw the Receptionist and left soon after. Dad took the train to work whilst Mum and I got a cab home. The journey was very quiet. The doctor's words played heavily on my mind. I could see that Mum didn't want to talk so I didn't bother her. She stared mindlessly outside the window whilst clutching my right hand like a toddler. The taxi driver took the longer route home—the 'scenic' route as we called it, passing by all the famous landmarks and busy streets of London. Embarking on journeys and travelling from place to place usually refreshed my mind, but not this one; the inside of the cab was as silent as a crypt.

Mum would always be Mum! I couldn't let her go. She was the permanent structure in my life. She was the pillar that kept us together; a piece of the puzzle that made us feel whole; an oak tree that stood its ground during storms and hurricanes; and the beat that kept the heart of this family alive. How could I let her go? How would we survive without her?

"It'll be ok, Mum. We'll find a way to get you treated," I reassured her. She put her hand over mine, but didn't say anything. It was like she was slowly bringing herself to accept that she might not make it.

We drove past the Bellington Hospital—the private hospital where Mum had her surgery the last time she had cancer, which also happened to be where they had the immunotherapy treatment that Dr Alan told us about. I knew how much Dad paid the last time, and there was no way we could afford that again. But I had to get her back there, I had to find a way to make some money to pay for her treatment.

Just then, as the taxi turned the next corner, I spotted a new bakery with bright glossy pictures of cookies and cakes covering the shop window. I remembered that strange dream I had—"Riya's Tasty Treats".

I closed my eyes and squeezed my eyelids against each other, trying hard to find a clue—a clue to unlock the message behind my dream, if there was one. Then, I realised, it finally made sense! I opened my eyes and smiled to myself.

That could be the answer, I thought. I knew what I had to do.

"I'm going to help you, Mum," I whimpered, turning to look at her face, "I promise! I know we can't afford private treatment at the moment, but I'm going to find us the money. I won't let you die." I pressed my lips against each other. I didn't want to cry in front of her.

"It's ok, darling, of course you will," she said in the way you would to silence a child. It didn't sound like she believed me. But I made myself a promise that I was going to live up to my words no matter what—I'd do whatever it took.

Chapter 5

'Tasty Treats'

We were still in the taxi when my mind flooded with a rainstorm of ideas. I was certain it was the right thing to do. I was good at baking things and everyone loved my cookies. Baking cookies and selling them at school was the best way for me to make money to help Mum.

As the taxi turned another corner, I thought excitedly about how much I could bake ready for when school opened again on Monday. I wasn't planning on selling the first hundred; instead, I was planning on giving them away for free to potential customers. That's the only bit of marketing I knew after seeing how *Mr Pretzels* drew in customers in Westfield's Shopping Centre.

The atmosphere in school around selling things was really tense because of the fierce competition, but I couldn't let that bother me. I had a mission to fulfil—a mission to save Mum. I had a fuller vision now, I needed to find the strength, I needed to become like a piece of metal, which expanded when heated by the high temperatures of stress, pressure and worry. I needed to focus all my energies on making enough money to get Mum treated.

Dark clouds gathered as the taxi parked at the entrance to our estate.

"I'm not going in there," said the driver, with the engine still running.

I looked up at him and stared at his round face as he scratched his overgrown greying stubble.

"Can you take us a bit closer to our block, please," I asked, "my Mum isn't well."

"I'm really sorry, love," he replied shaking his head, "I'd love to but the kids in these estates are crazy, they chuck all sorts of things at us. That's why us cabbies don't go in. I went into one a couple of weeks ago and my cab almost got smashed up, I can't have that! This is my bread and butter!"

As we got out of our taxi, Mum paid our fare and we walked into the Southern Estate where our block was. I looked to the left, beyond the endless rows of cement buildings to see another new build boarded up and covered with scaffolds slowly emerging into the sky. It felt like it was on a completely different island. *If only the council gave us a permanent home in one of those! I wish!*

In the corner of my eye, I noticed what looked like a heated argument taking place between some familiar and unfamiliar faces at the entrance past the rusty iron gates. It quickly turned physical with fists, boots and even bottles flying everywhere. Luckily, it didn't last long. Somebody yelled from one of the nearby tower blocks and the skirmish of boys quickly dispersed in different directions like cockroaches. Things like this always happened here; there was always tension and trouble between boys and girls from different estates.

"Come on, Riya, let's get inside," said Mum as her eyes followed two of the boys who slowly disappeared into the distance. I felt Mum's cold fingertips against my palms as she tried to find my hand.

"I'm here, Mum," I told her, tightening my grip on her hand.

It was getting dark and standing around outside wasn't safe at this time, anything could happen, so we paced home as quickly as we could.

I called Anisa to tell her about my idea the next day.

"Are you sure you wanna do this?" she asked. "You know Tooth Fairy Syed and Stacy pretty much run the show when it comes to selling stuff at school. Those two throw their weight around so other people can't make as much money as they do. You might run into them, have you thought about that?"

"I know, Anisa, but I don't have a choice. If I don't do this, Mum could die! That's the reality." When I told Anisa what Mum's doctor said to us about the new treatment that was only available privately, she seemed to understand.

"Sure, I'll help you, babe. Just let me know what you want me to do."

"By the way, why do they call Syed the 'Tooth Fairy'?" I asked, my mind racing back to what Harith told me about Syed's sneaky behaviour.

"I heard he used to attend Miss Winter's after school karate classes when he was a lot younger," she replied, "apparently he got his nickname after punching out the front teeth of one of his opponents during training."

"Seriously?" I gasped, "that poor guy who lost his teeth! Great—now I have to watch out for him and Stacy too!"

"Yeah, he does look really mean with that horrible face and those big bushy caterpillar eyebrows."

"So that's why nobody messes with him! I wish I continued with my karate lessons, but I was never the fighting type... plus studies got in the way," I told her.

"Oh yeah, I remember you said you used to do martial arts. You definitely should have continued."

"I wish I did."

"We need to be careful, babe, and you'll have to plan it properly. I mean work out the costs, see how much you need for your Mum's treatment, subtract the cost of ingredients, see how many cookies you can shift per day over the three days we're allowed to sell and then work out the profits."

"I'll do that," I agreed, "just need to get my head together."

"You're a clever girl, Riya, I'm sure you'll make it work."

I wish I had that much faith in myself. But in reality, I didn't have a choice; I needed to make it work, for Mum's sake!

I had enough ingredients at home for about 50 cookies. I wanted to start with those just to test the waters the next morning. I got Mum to help me mix the cookie dough, put them out onto three trays and bake them. I told her we had a baking competition at school. She didn't really ask any questions—I'm sure her mind was busy with other more important things.

The next morning, I carefully placed the cookies into my school bag. Wrapped in cling film, they sat inside two of Mum's biscuit tins. I sprayed my school bag with deodorant to disguise the strong scent of the freshly baked cookies, which was wafting out of the bag—I didn't want to walk around smelling like a bakery!

Anisa was already there waiting to help. Just as I was about to divide up the cookies between us, I saw Mr Phillips looking around with his beady eyes. He pretended to look past us, but for some reason, I felt him watching us when I looked away. I shrugged it off and didn't give it much thought. After all, I didn't have any time to waste.

"Right, we'll divide up the cookies between us," I told Anisa as I stuffed her side bag with individually wrapped cookies.

"Be careful, you'll break them." Anisa inhaled the rich aroma.

"Handle them with care," I said, "it's all about presentation."

"Don't worry!" she laughed, "you always were a perfectionist."

"Anisa, you focus on the garden area where the Year 7s and 8s are and I'll focus on the North Playground so I can distribute to other year groups including the sixth formers," I told her. "Don't charge anyone. Just hand them out to everyone who comes your way and tell them, if you want more, we'll be selling every Monday, Wednesday and Friday mornings."

"Don't charge? You mean we're going to all this effort to give out free cookies?" Anisa looked at me confused.

"Yes, free," I said, "that's how you lure in the customers—basic marketing, girl, come on!"

"So what do I get after giving out all these cookies?" she asked.

"You can have a free one," I said, smiling.

Anisa seemed unsure of my plan, but I knew she trusted me. We got to work and within an hour almost all of the carefully wrapped cookies were given out.

I was confident that the freshly baked cookies would be an instant hit—the fact that I'd sell them for 50 pence and that they still smelt fresh when they got to school gave me a huge advantage over the school canteen who were selling their hard, overbaked cookies for 65 pence. My cookies were also better quality than the other sellers who bought reduced stock from supermarkets.

50 x 50p would give me a total of just £25 per day. If I sold on our allocated three days, I could make about £75 by the end of the week. Subtract the cost of the ingredients and I'd probably be in profit of about £60—not bad for a start, but I knew it wouldn't be enough; surely private hospitals charge a lot more! Doing the figures made my efforts to sell fifty cookies a day seem worthless. *How would I ever make enough money to pay for Mum's treatment?* I needed to find a way to bake and sell a lot more.

I heard Dad's footsteps later that evening. I peered out of the living room and caught a glimpse of him walking in with a big paper bag. *It was Monday evening so he must have paid a visit to the local food bank,* I thought to myself.

I was anxiously waiting to hear about his enquiries with the Bellington Hospital so I could plan ahead and try to help him, but I knew he didn't like talking about money in front of me, so I waited by the kitchen door hoping he would bring it up in conversation with Mum. My ears were on high alert as I tiptoed around the small passage that was between our kitchen and the living room. I heard Dad taking things out of the paper bag and placing them inside the kitchen cupboards. He then sat on a chair by the kitchen table whilst Mum warmed his dinner for him in the microwave. I peeped through the door and into the kitchen. He had a newspaper in his hand, which he quickly glossed over. Mum placed his food on the table along with a glass of water. He fanned the steaming plate of rice and vegetables with his newspaper. My stomach tightened up as I waited for him to say something.

"Did you call them, love?" Mum finally asked, standing by the cooker.

"Yeah, I did." He took two spoonfuls of his food followed by two small sips of water before letting out a sigh. "I'll sort it, the money for the treatment I mean. I've made an appointment with the bank to apply for a new loan."

"You can't, darling. We're up to our eyeballs in debt already and what if this landlord gives us notice to leave, what are we gonna have left for a deposit if we need to relocate again?" She placed her hand on his shoulder.

"I'm bidding every week and we're still on the waiting list, so there's still hope for somewhere permanent!"

"I don't want you to get into more debt to pay for private treatment." Mum placed her hands on her face and let out a deep sigh. "I know you're under a lot of pressure already."

"Then what do you want me to do?" he snapped, "I can't just sit by and watch you..." He let out a deep sigh.

"I'm starting the chemo in a couple of weeks, we'll just see how I get on with that."

"No!" He banged his fist against the table. "You heard what the doctor said, the chances of recovery on chemo alone are next to none."

"The bank won't lend us any more money, my love, we have no choice." Mum stood up and placed her hands on the back of Dad's neck.

I couldn't stand there listening in anymore. I burst into the kitchen.

"I'll get the money, Dad, just tell me how much we need!"

Dad looked up at Mum with a confused look on his face. I hadn't rehearsed anything in my head; I said whatever came to mind.

"Dad, I don't want to lose Mum, I can't bear the thought of it! I want to help. I know we can't afford private healthcare for her and you did so well with that last time, but this time I want to help!"

"Riya, darling, I know it's gonna be hard, but... I really don't want to talk to you about this now, I..." He sighed and stopped for a bit, trying to hold back his tears. I'd obviously caught them off guard, but we didn't have much time; we needed to have this discussion. I needed to get it out there, I needed them both on board with my plan.

He quickly composed himself and tried to continue, but before he could, I cut in.

"Mum, Dad, I knew you guys wouldn't agree... but you see I've started to..." The words became muddled in my head, but I had their attention now—they both stared at me with blank faces.

Dad took off his glasses and blinked twice, adjusting his vision. He rubbed his temples and ran his fingers through his scruffy, uncombed hair and scratched his unkempt stubble. With their vision locked onto me like a homing device, Mum swallowed and looked at me hard whilst Dad bit his bottom lip. Maybe they didn't expect to hear what I was going to say next.

"I'm planning on selling cookies. Other sixth formers at school sell loads of things to make money. So with the help of Anisa, we've been 'testing the waters' at school and we've had a lot of interest from potential customers."

"Customers?" he said, sounding confused. "Anisa—was this her idea?" he asked. I could hear the annoyance in his tone.

"No, Dad, it was my idea," I replied quickly.

"Riya, we send you to school so you can do well, get some qualifications and get a headstart in life. To be the things and do the things that your Mum and I couldn't." He shook his head. Mum looked disappointed too.

"Customers?" he repeated, "you make it sound like you've started a business. Why, honey? Don't I give you money to spend every week? I know you and your brothers get free school meals, but I always give you a little more to top you up. Is that not enough?" He seemed to be getting a little upset. Mum kept silent.

"No, Dad, of course it is," I said, taking his hand in mine. "Dad, I know how hard you work to give us a better life. I'm not talking about that, I'm talking about Mum. She needs treatment, Dad, and I want to help."

"Riya, I can't deal with this now, I'm really tired. I've got an early shift tomorrow, I'm going to bed."

Dad stood up and walked off, his unfinished food still on the kitchen table. Mum gave me an emotionless smile and followed him. I didn't know how they were going to react, but I guess a kind of no reaction was good for now. *Dad obviously needed to sleep on it,* I thought to myself.

The following morning, I watched Dad iron his uniform. I didn't say anything to him. I sat there with my bowl of cereal. Mum gave me a wink and went to the living room to keep an eye on the little ones. I didn't know what that wink meant, but somehow I thought it meant everything was going to be OK. I anxiously waited for Dad to say something.

"Dad," I sighed, "please say something, anything!" The silence was killing me.

"Fine," he replied. "But if you wanna do this, I'm gonna help you. I'll buy the ingredients and give your Mum a hand with the dough mix when I come back from work. Let me know what days and when so we can get everything ready for you to bake the following morning. But you have to be careful; I can't have you getting distracted from your studies."

"Thanks, Dad. I knew you'd understand." He looked at me half-smiling before I ran over to give him a big hug. He knew it couldn't be helped. I knew he felt helpless, but wanted to do whatever he could to get Mum treated.

"I still need to go to the bank so I can pay for the upfront costs to start her treatment, but after that, if you can make around £100 every week that would be a great help. I'll add to it so we can pay for the treatment every week," he said reluctantly. "God, why am I even asking you? I should be handling it myself," he muttered to himself as he sighed and shook his head.

£100 a week? I muttered to myself, *how was I going to make £100 a week by selling only three days per week?* I knew selling in school alone wouldn't be enough, I needed to find other ways to sell more cookies, but I didn't say anything to Mum or Dad.

"It's fine, Dad," I lied, "I can manage, I want to help, we need to get Mum's treatment started as soon as possible."

I breathed a sigh of relief knowing that I had both Mum and Dad on board, but I still needed to plan everything in detail if I was going to have any success in helping Dad pay for Mum's treatment.

I'll deal with it, I whispered to myself. *I can handle it, I have to!*

Chapter 6

We're in Business!

I got up really early the next morning and heard Dad on the phone to Bellington Hospital before he went to work. He made an appointment with them to take Mum in for an initial consultation with a plan to start treatment in two weeks after her chemotherapy started up again.

I didn't want to waste any time. I had enough dough for another fifty cookies. I placed the balls of dough onto a baking tray and slipped it into the oven. After about twenty minutes they turned into beautiful light brown cookies. I packed them into an empty biscuit tin and headed out.

Once I got through the school gates by 7:30, cookies and money exchanged hands very quickly. I placed ten individually wrapped cookies in the pockets of both sides of my jacket. Each time I saw someone make eye contact with me and give me the "nod", I knew what they wanted. I slowly made my way to them, carefully taking out a cookie from my pocket and placing it firmly into their clearly visible blazer pocket. We remained close to each other until cash exchanged hands. I then casually walked away to my next customer. There was no particular order or pattern I used to sell and distribute my stock in the playground, but I didn't want to alert Tooth Fairy Syed or Stacy who were always patrolling both sides of the playground even though they usually sold during lunch times. They didn't even stick to Mondays, Wednesdays and Fridays, which were the allocated days for us Year 13s. Syed and Stacy sold on whatever days they wanted, which wasn't fair on the Year 12s who sold their goods on Tuesdays and Thursdays, but everyone was too scared to say anything.

Most students paid for two cookies, others bought three or sometimes four—they were quick to get them before they sold out and some students even paid the early comers to buy on their behalf so they could eat them when they got in a little later and just before morning registration. By 8:15 am, my entire stock was gone and I made £25 mostly in £1 and 50 pence coins.

I was relieved but I knew I had another problem to fix; our small cooker at home wasn't big enough to make as many cookies as I needed. It didn't help that it was old and the oven gave off a funny smell. I was afraid it would break down. I knew Dad wouldn't be able to replace it, so I needed somewhere else to bake my cookies.

The demand was there, but how was I going to continue baking? I was racking my brains, I couldn't think of another way to bake my cookies. I couldn't ask Anisa. She was already helping me out and I couldn't possibly put a burden on her cooker too—what would her parents think?

As the playground was emptying, I saw two students collapse by the drinking fountains—they looked like Year 7 students. Staff who were on duty rushed towards them and sat them up—both students were holding vape pens! I knew it, more and more students were putting that rubbish into their lungs! *What do they put in them that's so strong that it causes such a reaction?* I wondered.

Miss Alford quickly rushed to the scene and ushered the remaining Year 7 students in for the morning registration before they started forming a large crowd in the playground. Miss Alford or Lindsay as I knew her then, briefly lived on the same block as us a couple of years ago. She came over from Canada to study here in the UK. I first met her when some of her mail was accidentally delivered to our address. She had beautiful, thick light brown hair and a wonderful smile, which lit up her eyes like it came from deep inside.

I think she was still at university then. We got on really well; she helped me with revision by teaching me good study habits and memory techniques. Lindsay was a down to earth person, but I lost contact with her after we moved, then one day I saw her at my school during the first year of my A-Levels. She'd finished off her teacher training and started working at my school. I couldn't call her Lindsay anymore; I had to call her Miss Alford. She became the Food Technology teacher.

I watched her curly hair bounce on her shoulders as she used both hands to guide her students in like an air steward.

I hope those two youngsters get back on their feet.

Just then an idea popped into my head.

That's it, I told myself. *That's the only way I can continue baking loads of cookies.*

I approached Miss Alford at break time. She was sitting in one of the break spaces with a thermal travel mug in one hand. I told her about Mum's situation.

She looked up at me sympathetically, her eyes a little watery.

"I had a mum once too," she sighed. "I used to always send money back home for her every month when she became very unwell. I lost her a few months ago."

Miss Alford was a lovely person. She lived locally and must have understood the difficulties facing families like mine. She wasn't detached from us like some of the other teachers were—she related to us like no one else could. She seemed to understand us and appeared more human. That's why I trusted her.

"OK, I'll help," she agreed. "You can use the ovens in the morning as long as you buy your own ingredients and bring in the cookie dough ready to bake. I get in really early anyway so I'll open up the Cooking Studio for you."

"Thanks, Miss, I really appreciate it."

"Make sure you don't tell anyone," she added, "otherwise everyone will accuse me of favouritism even though our Principal supports this 'entrepreneurial streak' as he calls it, amongst some of the Sixth Formers."

"No one will know, Miss, I promise."

"And keep out of Mr Phillips's radar," she added.

"Mr Phillips, the Business and Economics teacher? What's he got to do with anything?" I asked.

"Nothing. I probably shouldn't have said anything," she replied, looking upwards towards the second floor where Mr Phillips's classroom was. "Let's just say he has his favourites," she added, "anyway, I've got to go." Miss Alford finished her coffee, grabbed her bag and left.

At lesson time, I switched off and focused on my learning—I didn't want that to suffer. I raced to finish all my work and even completed parts of any homework when the teacher gave us a "ten-minute breather" during the double lessons.

I always had one or two cookies left every day so at break times, I walked around the school to find Lucy so I could give her the leftover cookies. I knew from the way Lucy dressed that she came from a family with very little money. Some of the other girls teased her and called her all sorts of names. If I saw them, I'd usually tell them to "get lost" and then slip two cookies into Lucy's pocket. She would try to politely refuse, but in the end, she would take them. Sometimes those cookies were all I saw her eat.

I easily sold my batch of cookies within thirty or so minutes, but Anisa was slightly slower, so when I finished, I had to work extra hard to sell all the remaining stock before the school day started.

Miss Alford let us use her ovens every morning as promised. The studio had huge extractor fans that sucked out the cooking smell so that it didn't travel to other parts of the school.

I stopped by our local post office on the way back from school, and used their money-changing machine to turn all the coins I had collected into bank notes.

A week and a half in and I was feeling exhausted.

"What's it all looking like, Annie?" I asked, looking at her searchingly. I felt bad about asking her to help in my mission even though she was my best friend. But she didn't complain, not to my face anyway!

"Well after the costs for the ingredients, accounting for the cookies you give away for free, you're left with

£110," she explained, tapping away at the calculator on her phone.

"That's really great, Annie," I smiled. "It will definitely help to pay for the first week of Mum's treatment once she gets started, but it's not enough, we need to find a way to sell more cookies!"

"We already sell a little over fifty per day Riya on our assigned three days," explained Anisa, "there just isn't enough time to sell any more than that." Her eyes stared at me for new ideas.

"I wonder if there's a way to bake some cookies to sell outside of school now that we've got Miss Alford's help?"

Anisa didn't say anything.

"Not as individual cookies," I explained, "but in bigger quantities for parties and events, like some people do on Instagram."

"Maybe," replied Anisa, although she didn't sound too convinced.

I was on my last leg by the time the weekend came. I spent the weekends resting and catching up on schoolwork. I also bought the ingredients for the following week's baking—I felt guilty relying on Dad all the time. I just needed to stay on top of things in my hectic life.

Chapter 7

Treatment Plan

The next morning, I slipped into Mum and Dad's bedroom while they were still sleeping. I placed the plastic bank notes from all the profits on the top of their chest of drawers and put Dad's mobile phone on top so the wind didn't blow it away before sneaking out of their room.

Even though we'd hit a milestone, I kept worrying about how I would sell enough cookies to make the £100 Dad needed every week to keep paying for Mum's treatment. I sat on the living room sofa lost in thought, when I heard Mum and Dad shuffling about in their room—*they must be up and getting ready.* I took a deep breath, forced myself up and went to my room to get changed. Today was a big day; today was the day we were taking Mum to the Bellington Hospital to set up her treatment plan.

Walking out of the estate, I noticed a few hoodlums looking at us menacingly, giving us their usual ugly stares. They made me feel very uncomfortable, so I ran ahead of Dad and quickly waved down a taxi. I looked back as we drove off, but they weren't looking at us anymore.

As our taxi approached the Bellington Hospital and pulled into the narrow entrance path, I saw a lot of other black taxis and some chauffeur-driven cars pull in before us. I saw drivers coming out and opening the doors for their passengers. Most walked out on foot, but a couple were helped out of a taxi and onto a wheelchair, which was conveniently tucked away in the boot of the car. White-gloved hospital porters were on standby, waiting to help the patients whenever they needed—at times simply extending a hand, other times walking the patient in and sometimes pushing a wheelchair or a portable chair for them. The white-gloved men looked very smart and were always smiling. *You would never see this in a regular hospital,* I thought to myself.

Looking up at the huge hospital sign made me happy. I knew we were very fortunate that we were getting Mum treated and I was really grateful. I thought of the people who couldn't afford this sort of care and stood no chance of recovery. Right underneath the hospital sign was the entrance. You couldn't help but notice two huge glass displays on either side of the entrance—on one side was a continuous artificial waterfall and on the other side stood a life-sized statue of a family cuddling up together as if they were about to pose for a portrait. It calmed my nerves. I heard the traffic behind me and cars pulling into the hospital, but for that moment, I completely zoned out. I remembered the moments of happiness and laughter we used to have when my younger brothers and I were a lot smaller—we didn't have moments like that these days. Even when we moved from place to place with no stability, we always had each other. Those thoughts gave me mixed feelings; I was comforted by them, but at the same time not knowing what the future held terrified me, especially the thought of possibly losing Mum. I looked up at the sky remembering how I prayed and pleaded to God for some help. I was sure this was part of the answer!

"Thank you," I whispered, "thank you so much!"

"Riya, hurry up. Let's get your mum registered so I can get to work on time." Dad grabbed my hand and pulled me towards him, breaking me out of my temporary trance.

Approaching the automatic glass doors, we went straight into the Reception area. The place must have had a refurbishment recently because it looked very different from the last time we were there; it always looked very pleasant, but for some reason, it looked even more beautiful now. The doors closed behind us, cutting off any noise from the outside together with the natural sunlight. We walked straight ahead on the shiny clean dark beige coloured floor tiles, which absorbed some of the sunlight from outside and reflected the soft light from the ceiling. The stunning lights were a perfect guide to a beautifully designed Reception area, which had thin black borders around a darker beige coloured reception table that looked like it was floating. Behind it stood men dressed in business-like suits and beside them was a very visible counter decorated with fresh flowers which offered patients tea, coffee, water and different juices.

"Good afternoon, sir, and welcome to the Bellington. Are you a paying patient or do you have an insurance policy?" asked one of the neatly dressed men in his very posh accent. He made eye contact with us all and maintained his smile throughout his entire conversation with Dad.

"Paying," said Dad.

"Very well, sir, I'll just need a few details so I can book the patient in." The Receptionist typed away at his keyboard and then raised his eyes at Dad.

Dad handed over an envelope of cash to the Receptionist, which he counted and then gave Dad a receipt before typing something on his computer again. They booked Mum in for an appointment the following day with consultant Dr Yiannis to decide what the best course of treatment for her would be. They also requested to read her most recent hospital reports before coming to an informed decision. The new experimental immunotherapy treatment would start the following Monday, which they said would most likely be twice a week on top of her chemotherapy sessions at St Christopher's Hospital.

At last, we were making progress. Finally, Mum was going to get some treatment that could cure her, however slim the chances were. Knowing that we were moving forward gave me the much-needed encouragement to carry on with my cookies. I'd do as I was doing—start the baking cycle every Monday, Wednesday and Friday morning and sell as many cookies as I could in school.

As we reached this important milestone, I couldn't help feeling that someone was looking over us; not a person, but a higher power who listened to my cries for help. I knew there was someone out there, beyond everything that I could physically see and touch. I'd felt feelings like this before, but this time was different and I was determined not to disregard them. There must be a purpose and reason behind everything, even the hardships in life, I thought to myself.

The following day I made my way home early straight after school. I wanted to get home whilst it was still daylight. It was a mildly cold afternoon and the stench from the slowly drying damp roads filled my nose. Striding home as quickly as I could, I saw strange figures slowly coming out in the distance near our block of flats just as the daylight was beginning to slowly disappear. I saw one boy race past me with his Mohican style haircut—sides shaved with a slab of hair drooping down the front of his skull, almost completely covering his left eye. I looked back to see him join a small group of boys who were waiting for him like a herd of sheep expecting one of their own to re-join the flock. Their voices became more distant as the gap between us grew bigger. Looking back a second time and adjusting my vision, I saw them staring straight back at me—but they quickly dispersed as a patrolling police car drove past.

Just then, I saw Nadim walking towards the front entrance to our estate. I stopped in my tracks, gazing at him from afar. He looked past me, but then his eyes returned for a second look. As he walked towards me, I noticed his glowing skin, his perfectly proportioned features and his ever-present smile, flashing his perfectly straight pearly teeth. He looked so handsome, almost good enough to eat!

"I thought I noticed you, Riya," he said, "why are you standing there? Why aren't you inside? It's freezing."

"I was just... I mean..." The words were stumbling inside my mouth again as I struggled to form a clear sentence. I couldn't tell him that I was standing there just because I saw him.

"I thought I dropped my hair clip," I lied.

"Oh, well, did you find it then?" he asked, his eyes scanning the floor near my feet.

"No, it doesn't matter, it's not a big deal," I replied trying not to look at his thick, neatly brushed lustrous black hair.

He came closer, his face inches away from mine, and his eyes were locked onto my hair. My heart began to race again. *I hope he can't hear the echoes of my beating heart.*

"Well I can see two hair clips still firmly there," he pointed, "how many do you usually wear?"

"It doesn't matter, Nadim, it's fine," I said awkwardly.

"Are you OK, Riya? You seem a bit distant," he said, scanning my face, moving from my eyes and lips.

I wanted to tell him, tell him everything I mean—from my worries about Mum to the stresses and strains of trying to sell baked cookies to help pay for her treatment, but I couldn't find the words. I looked at the swings in the children's playground on my left.

"Nadim, can we... I mean..." My throat dried up, the words were stuck again.

"What is it, Riya, do you need help with something?" His wide puppy dog eyes had me in a trance. My brain and body started to hurt from pretending everything was OK, but I couldn't gather the courage to open up to him.

"I've got a History assignment due quite soon and I haven't even made a start on it." I felt a stab of guilt as I tried to sound convincing. There was no point telling him about my problems and worries, and I definitely couldn't tell him about the weird feelings I got every time he was around—I didn't even understand them myself.

"I'm sure you'll get it done on time, Riya," he replied, "if not, I'm sure you can ask for an extension."

"Yeah, maybe." My eyes fell to the ground as I stared mindlessly at the tiny amount of space between myself and Nadim.

"Are you sure there's nothing else, Riya? I mean you're always on top of things, you don't seem like the type to worry about not meeting a deadline, you're way cleverer than me!"

"It's just been a busy week that's all. I'll try and get it done on time."

"I'm sure it will be fine. Anyway, gotta shoot off, see you in school."

As we both parted, I turned around to look at him again, he turned too and waved as he fixed his earbuds into both ears.

I continued walking until I passed through the entrance to our estate. I looked to my left where the new block of expensive-looking posh flats was starting to take shape; its black and grey brickwork was clearly visible. I could see a small group of people protesting at the bottom of the building; they held out various placards—I couldn't see them clearly. They were probably local people complaining about the lack of housing for local residents despite the council allowing big companies to build these huge fancy-looking flats—that's what most people protested about in this area. Not that it made any difference! I walked on, shutting out the faint voices of the protesters as I approached our block.

When I got home, Mum was lying on the living room sofa and Aakil and Aahan were playing with their toy cars. I ran to my bedroom, kicked off my sweaty clothes after pouring myself a glass of lemon iced tea. I ran myself a hot bath, poured some almond milk and honey calming bath pearls into the hot water, and then mixed in some cold water until it was a perfect temperature. With my drink carefully resting on the side, I climbed in and dipped my entire body into the caressing water. The smells shot up my nose and I tasted the strong aroma of milk and honey.

I tensed my body and then exhaled to relax. I got comfortable admiring the oily texture of my body as the soapy bath water danced on my skin. I lay still—this was my escape. For a few moments I forgot about the troubles of life; Mum's illness, my struggles to make enough money to help Dad get her treated, keeping on top of my studies, taking care of the house and the two little ones; and not seeing much of Dad because he had to work even on his rest days.

Chapter 8

The Clash

It was the day of our weekly assembly. I stopped what I was doing for a moment and I looked up to the sky and then around the playground. The sun sent out bright rays of light across the turf and there were loud chatters from students who were rushing around as the bell sounded. The soft golden heat caressed my face as I looked up and inhaled the warm air, but there was no time to pause; I had to finish selling my batch of cookies quickly as time was closing in on me. I washed my hands at the drinking fountains, sprayed myself with perfume and quickly paced towards where the other sixth formers were lining up to enter the main hall. I saw Anisa also falling in line, fixing her *hijab* and straightening her long black skirt.

"Coats off, and bags by your sides please. Look sharp, look smart and be ready to enter the hall," shouted Mr Cord, our Second in Charge of Sixth Form, in his slightly raised monotone voice whilst handing out registers to the form teachers.

That's a bit strange, no Mr Gorton? He usually did this part while Mr Cord prepared the inside of the hall, but I looked in to see Mr Phillips ordering the premises staff around inside. *What was he doing there? He's not even one of those older important teachers even though I'm sure he wanted to be!*

"OK, in we get," were Mr Cord's final instructions as the form tutors struggled to take registers while the students were on the move—it was a bit like trying to spot someone on a slow-moving train. As we sat down in rows, he did what Mr Gorton usually did on the Wednesday morning assembly: give a short motivational speech, which I'm sure was made up, give out some awards, and then yell at us all for our lack of motivation. He did all of that like a robot. In fact, if I wasn't looking straight at him, I'd think it was Mr Gorton speaking out of Mr Cord's body. But nothing prepared me for his next announcement:

"You may have noticed that Mr Gorton isn't present," he said, with a mild frown on his face, "unfortunately he's had to leave suddenly due to personal reasons." I noticed a change in his usual measured tone of voice. It sounded like he was reluctant to make this announcement, but had to. He coughed, clearing his throat to continue.

Personal reasons, I thought to myself? What does that mean? It could mean anything! But why would Mr Gorton, the Head of Sixth Form, suddenly leave without saying goodbye to us and wishing us good luck? That didn't seem like him and anyway, I thought teachers usually left at the end of the term, not right in the middle of one. Something smelled fishy, but I didn't know what. Well, since Mr Cord was the Second in Charge, he'd just take over I guess.

"I am pleased to announce that Mr Phillips will be your new Head of Sixth Form and I will of course continue to work closely with him as your Second in Charge of Sixth Form," he finished, trying to start a round of applause, but a deafening silence filled the hall apart from a few claps from some students sitting in the front row.

Everyone froze in their seats. We weren't exactly huge fans of Mr Phillips—he always came across as a bit arrogant with his chest stuck out and back as straight as an ironing board every time he walked past you. Then I remembered what Miss Alford said about him. Something was definitely wrong with this whole thing. How did Mr Phillips jump straight from being a regular teacher to Head of Sixth Form?

"Thank you, Mr Cord," he said, rubbing his hands like a cheeky prankster. "I just wanted to say that I'm very happy to be your Head of Sixth Form. I hear that you are hardworking and well-behaved, so I feel very privileged to be in such good company. One of my first objectives as your Head of Sixth Form will be to refocus my year group to learning and academic achievement, which is why you are here." He stared into the crowd and looked around with a sly smirk on his face as the Sixth Formers started muttering amongst themselves.

I looked around at everyone, most of whom were staring at Mr Phillips with blank faces. I tried to find Anisa in the crowd, but I couldn't spot her. Then I looked back at the Sixth Form teachers who were standing at the back, who all looked gloomy and were muttering something amongst themselves too. I could see one teacher shaking her head.

What on earth is going on? What's he up to?

I had so many questions flying around inside my head. I looked back at the podium where Mr Phillips was standing.

"I'd like to have your attention please," he demanded, holding out his right hand like a traffic warden.

"Oh, what now?" I muttered to myself.

"I am sure you are all aware that our new Principal, Mr Faulkner is supportive of some of our Sixth Form students selling food items on the school premises," he continued, "however, I feel that some of you are becoming distracted by all of this. That's why I am going to allow only a select number of students to sell specific things at clearly defined times."

The students' voices became louder; I could hear the screeching sounds of their chairs against the old wooden floors.

"I will be implementing the new rules in the coming weeks and my Sixth Form Associates Team will keep a close eye until my plans are finalised," he added, slightly raising his voice and pointing at a few students who were sitting on the front row. Syed was amongst them. He sat up, straightened his back and looked around with a sneering smile.

So those lot are his Sixth Form Associates clan.

He finished off his speech before handing it back to Mr Cord who dismissed us from the back, row by row.

I didn't understand, why didn't he say anything about those who were selling vape pens in the school? *Why was he so hell-bent on limiting the students that sold cookies, crisps and doughnuts? Surely this was a serious case of misplaced priorities!*

As I walked out of the assembly, I saw Tooth Fairy Syed and Stacy giving me ugly stares whilst mumbling amongst themselves. I looked up to see the clouds twisting and transforming into dangerous metallic grey blobs streaked with silver. It was still bright and sunny, but I could tell it wasn't going to last very long. Mr Phillips' announcement definitely put a "spanner in the works", just when I was getting the hang of things. I didn't understand why he was doing this. We operated relatively openly, but now his new plans were going to affect me, I needed a new strategy.

I bumped into Anisa in the playground after the assembly.

"What was all that about?" I asked, scratching my head. "Have you heard any gossip? Why did Mr Gorton suddenly leave without saying anything?

"I don't know for sure," she replied, "but I overheard some of the other teachers saying he was pushed out after they found something in one of his cupboards."

"Like what?" I asked, frowning. "Mr Gorton is a decent guy."

"Whatever it was, it was something he shouldn't have had. I don't know how true it is though."

"What?" My eyes lit up. "What do you mean? Mr Gorton is one of the kindest teachers in this whole school—firm but fair. What could he possibly have had in his school cupboard?" Something didn't seem right, and I felt almost angry at the injustice.

"Anisa, we need to be extra vigilant and continue to sell—I still need the money," I cautioned, "nothing's changed! God knows what Mr Phillips is up to with that announcement!"

"We'll carry on as we are," she replied, "until things change that is. It's almost time for the first lesson, we better hurry."

"I'll see you up there," I told her, "I need to get to the lockers and get my Russian Revolution textbook."

Anisa raced ahead to class while I made the short walk to the Sixth Form lockers area, which was slowly beginning to empty. I quickly took out my textbook and notepad, and held them in my hand after placing the rest of my belongings inside the locker. As I was closing the door to my locker, leaning against it stood a tall bulky figure; it was Tooth Fairy Syed. His arms were crossed in front of his chest, which he pushed forward and locked his eyes onto me. I noticed the clenched straight jaw-bones on his sour face. As he moved closer to me, I could smell his strong aftershave. It made me feel sick!

"Can I help you with something?" I asked, taking a deep breath. I shut my locker and turned my key to close it, resting my left hand on the locker door.

"Nope," he replied swiftly, "but maybe we can help each other." He passed his index finger over my left hand, feeling my knuckles. I yanked my hand back quickly.

I looked around; nobody else was there—it was just me and him in a tight square-shaped locker room that was no bigger than two or three toilet cubicles. He moved even closer. I could feel his warm breath on my face.

"No need to be jumpy," he smirked, "I thought we could get to know each other first."

"Sorry, but I don't think you can help me with any-thing," I replied politely, trying to get past, but he didn't even flinch. He stood in front of the small gap between me and the exit door.

"Listen here, little girl," he continued, his voice was deep and cold, "you've been selling cookies, and I've heard they're very popular. But no one sells anything in this school without paying us a fee." A cheeky smile ap-peared on his face.

"What 'fee'?" I looked up into his eyes.

"At the moment, it's 30% of your weekly takings, which might rise to 50% by the time Mr Phillips brings his new rules in."

"You can't do that, that's not fair." I grit my teeth.

"That's the rules we Sixth Form Associates are setting now that Mr Gorton is out of the picture. If you can't pay, I'll make sure you have no customers, believe me—my powers of persuasion are pretty good," he sniggered.

"And where is this money going, the 'fee' I mean?"

"That's not for you to know, but if you can't pay the fee cos you're short on cash, why don't you team up with me and I'm sure you can make four times as much as you're making now. You just have to change your product a little, but carry on working as hard as you do—I've heard you've built quite a customer base!"

"What do you mean, change my product?" I asked. "My cookies are doing fine thanks."

"You're a talented girl, I'm sure you can sell other popular things that are in demand. I need more hard workers to shift my stuff."

"What stuff?" I frowned. "I'm fine selling my cookies thank you, I don't want to work for you!"

"Keep your voice down, little girl." He looked around. "I'm giving you an opportunity here."

"What's to stop me from going to the Principal to tell him you've been intimidating me?"

"This is a private conversation between me and you," he laughed, "nobody else here—my word against yours!" he grinned exposing his stained teeth.

"I don't want anything to do with whatever you're selling," I snapped. "Now if you'll excuse me, I need to get to lesson."

"What about your friend, that hot *hijabi* babe? I'm sure she'll be interested in making a little money on the side—university fees aren't cheap next year!"

"Leave Anisa out of this," I demanded, "she's just helping out a friend!"

"Suit yourself, just thought I'd share the love, bring you in," he muttered as I brushed past him and made my way to lesson. I don't know what disgusted me more; his sleazy attitude or his menacing behaviour.

Chapter 9

Head-on Collision!

My encounter with Syed was playing on my mind all day. I didn't tell Anisa—I didn't want to scare her or stress her out. I tried to put my thoughts and fears aside and carry on as normal.

As the pips sounded to indicate the end of break, I stood at the bottom of the North Staircase and took a deep breath before running my fingers through my hair. I placed the cold palms of my hands on my face for a few seconds to try to calm my nerves and keep focused. I closed my eyes, allowing the cold tips of my fingers to softly press against my eyelids like two cold slices of cucumber. The feeling was soothing.

My warm face started to heat up my permanently cold hands. It was time to wake myself up and get on with the rest of the day, but just as I opened my eyes, I saw her. I adjusted my vision and there she was again. She grabbed me by my shirt and lifted me all the way up to her face. I was on the tips of my toes and felt my shirt tighten around my back as she twisted her clenched grip clockwise and anti-clockwise to get a better hold of me. Her face was right up against mine. I smelt her breath and the cheap lip gloss that was smudged around her lips. She gritted her teeth and twisted her mouth a thousand different ways. At first, I didn't recognise her because she was so close to me, but then I made the connection—it was Stacy from my year group! Stacy, who always seemed attached to Syed's hip. With her short blonde hair tied in a simple ponytail, she looked at me hard, with her blood-shot red eyes almost popping out of her head. I thought she was going to hurt me; she easily could, there was no one else around. The pips had already sounded and the students were all inside the main building. I was the only one there near the staircase facing the North Dining Area.

"Not so smart are you?" she whispered in my left ear whilst tightening her grip even more. "I know what you're up to. Who do you think you are, selling cookies with your little friend? You must think you're so clever!" She sucked her teeth at me wildly. "Because of you and your little friend, I haven't been able to sell anything for weeks—it means I have to sell even more of that..." she stopped herself abruptly. "Every day, I'm giving stuff away for free to attract customers," she shouted. Her bark was so loud it temporarily made me deaf in one ear. For a few seconds, I couldn't hear what she was saying. All I could hear was a ringing sound. "Well, let me tell you this, Miss Smarty Pants," she continued. "I'm gonna bring you down and your little friend. I know people who will slap some sense into you!"

I felt the blood rushing to my head; I could feel the heat in my eyes as I blinked rapidly, trying to make sense of what was going on. The pressure in my head was boiling up like a kettle and my eyes started to feel blurry; I almost lost my composure. I felt the panic rising in my chest. I took a deep breath and swallowed hard. I had to quickly find myself again and think on my feet.

"Well you've just physically assaulted me," I replied, exhaling.

"Yeah, is that right?" she smirked, "who you gonna run to anyway? Mr Phillips," she scoffed, "I'm one of his Sixth Form Associates now, he'll believe me over you anytime!"

"I'll go to our Principal, Mr Faulkner, he's still the boss of everyone, including Mr Phillips," I replied, "and I don't think he takes a liking to big bullies like you!" This sudden realisation made her push me towards the wall, letting go of my shirt.

Stacy pulled back into a momentary pause. She stood still, moving her eyes in every direction, trying to respond.

"OK, Miss Smarty Pants," she nodded, "don't think you're too smart yeah, I'm watching you and I'll find a way to get you. Soon you'll be finished in this school!" she shouted aggressively, pulling back her hands and trying to prevent them from going for my throat. "Wait till I've spoken to Syed!"

I let out a long sigh of relief as she let me go and walked off. I adjusted my top and headed straight for my lesson.

I sat in lesson completely shaken up; I was there in body only; my mind was busy with millions of thoughts buzzing around inside my head about what just happened. I sat at my table, mindlessly taking notes from the whiteboard while my brain was trying to digest the things Stacy said to me. *What did she mean by "it means I have to sell even more of that..."? Why didn't she finish her sentence? What was she trying to hide and why?*

Chapter 10

New Strategies

I didn't know what Stacy and Syed were up to, but I knew I needed to continue selling cookies in school even though it wasn't enough to make the £100 Dad needed every week. To make up for the shortfall, I decided to have a go at selling some of my cookies outside of school.

I started doing a little bit of advertising—mostly around local parks, playgroups, supermarkets and anywhere else I thought I could stick one of my A5 flyers that I ordered through the internet. I put my name and number on the glossy flyer with the heading: *Riya's Tasty Treats*. Within the first week, I started to get a few small orders at a time. I couldn't handle any more than one or two local orders every other day otherwise it would be too much for me. News of my cookies slowly spread and I was getting one or two orders every few days. I couldn't ask Anisa to help me after school after all the help she was already giving in school on Mondays, Wednesdays and Fridays.

This new challenge meant, when I got an order, I had to bake another 30–40 cookies straight after school and then jump onto my bike to be able to deliver them.

I baked the cookies in Miss Alford's studio—she usually worked late marking books and was kind enough to let me use her ovens even after school. I sealed them in individual paper bags, placed them into two of Mum's biscuit tins, then put the tins into my school bag and made my way to deliver them. I delivered the cookies, collected the money, and made my way home.

Even though I had very few orders after school, they still put another strain on me. I already felt drained and fatigued. *How would I continue this life?* I was tired and exhausted. I knew I couldn't sustain this; I had to focus on selling inside school despite the risks of running into Syed and Stacy—I couldn't rely on the occasional outside orders that I got.

Within a few days, Mr Phillips' gang were everywhere! I saw his little cronies through the clear small glass pane of his classroom window each time I walked past. His Sixth Form Associates met him on most mornings as part of their "enrichment"—I'm sure they wanted to get in his good books before the university applications started. These handpicked "pets" had special badges clearly visible on their jackets and enjoyed privileges like not having to queue up for lunch and being able to go out of the school at lunch times twice a week. He picked his "henchmen" very carefully, always focusing on those who looked up to him, wanted to impress him or students that he knew were desperate to make money in school. He knew how to use people, manipulate them and get them to do what he wanted.

Most of Mr Phillips's clique weren't that bad, but Tooth Fairy Syed was the most arrogant and intimidating of them all. He was always hanging around Mr Phillips, trying to impress him in any way he could. I don't know what was in it for him, but he did whatever Mr Phillips asked him to do. He was also partnered with Stacy—*what a horrible team!*

Whatever that alliance meant, I tried to embrace this external challenge. I tried to see it as an opportunity to grow and develop my plans, but deep down I was scared, always looking over my shoulder to see if anyone was watching me, especially Syed and Stacy!

At first, I thought there was no need to be greedy as there were plenty of customers to go around, so I assumed that everyone would just get on with it, but I was wrong— there was always rivalry between different sellers. I tried to keep busy and not let the competition side distract me from my mission. I was focused; I kept track of the baking, selling and taking in the profits at the end of each day, whilst at the same time keeping an eye out for any after school orders, which were very slow.

I came home to find Mum struggling to sit upright on the living room sofa. She covered her legs with a white blanket and sat with a cup of tea in one hand and the TV remote in the other. I saw her fighting to keep herself awake with tea and TV. It wasn't working though, her eyes were drooping and she was shaking like her clothes weren't enough to keep herself warm. She was trying to hide it, but I felt the small vibrations on the sofa when I sat next to her. She was always like this on treatment days—it took a lot out of her. They took place once a month during the weekdays. I tried to go with her when Dad couldn't get the time off, but there were a few times when no one could go with her. On those days, she had to board the hospital transport bus by herself. Even though I knew they would pick her up and drop her off, I still found myself worrying about her. *What if something happened to her? What if she fainted? What if she fell trying to board the bus? What if, what if?* My mind was always full of endless questions so I constantly texted her in between my lessons. Sometimes she replied quickly, but at other times she took ages to reply, which made me worry even more.

Even though this new purpose allowed me to realign my focus and attention, I started to feel fragile inside. I needed to find myself, find my strength, but I didn't know where to look to find it. I thought about Anisa and how happy, relaxed and carefree she seemed at times—I wished I could be like that. I definitely needed to be, but I didn't know where to find the strength from.

Chapter 11

New Inspirations

The next day at break time, I went to look for Lucy so I could slip her a couple of leftover cookies. I walked into the library and scanned my eyes around, but couldn't see her anywhere, so I slumped on a chair on one of the empty tables. I decided to sit for a few minutes just to clear my head. As I turned to my right, in the corner of the library hidden behind the non-fiction section, I saw Lucy sitting on one of the comfy chairs. She had her head stuck in a book with a colourful blue cover with lots of pictures on it; it caught my attention so I walked towards her.

"What are you reading?" I asked Lucy, handing her the two cookies left over from the morning. She handed the book over, said "thanks" and left. I picked it up and glossed over it; *A Brief Illustrated Guide to Islam* by I. A. Ibrahim. It looked really interesting, I felt inclined to at least read the first chapter, which was about the Oneness of God (Allah in Arabic); how He is the only one worthy of worship without any partners. I couldn't help myself; I quickly moved to the second chapter. It was about the Prophet Muhammad (peace be upon him); his simple life, his honesty, his truthfulness, his integrity, his mission and the struggles that came with it. Before I knew it, the pips sounded again and it was time to go to lesson. Islam

fascinated me, the simplicity of it and how so many people like my friend Anisa were so faithful to the religion. I
handed it over to the librarian at the desk who scanned
the barcode and handed it back. I slipped it into my bag
and rushed to lesson.

Over the next few days, I kept the book in my bag—
reading a chapter here and there whenever I got a spare
moment. I didn't tell anyone, not even Anisa. The more I
read about Islam—its justice, the charity, how it elevat-
ed the rights of women and how there was a loving and
beneficent God, the more I felt pulled towards it. It made
me think about everything; life, death, Mum's illness, but
there were still some things that I wanted to know more
about, like how such a simple faith can be practised by so
many different people in different parts of the world? I
tried not to think about it too much. *Maybe things will get
clearer as I read on.*

I tried to drop some questions to Anisa in a subtle way
so she didn't notice that I was reading about her religion.

"Islam is such a straightforward religion, but how do
you know if you're getting it right?" I asked, "There is so
much to learn."

"Yeah, you're right," she replied, "like the *hijab* for
example. It's not just a piece of cloth you place on your
head, you're supposed to wear it with modest loose-fit-
ting clothing that covers you properly!"

"I've seen it done differently by different people," I
commented.

"A *hijab* sometimes takes time, girls need to feel comfortable with it—it takes a while before someone is able to
embrace the *hijab* fully and match it with modest clothing
that suits their tastes."

"So it's about being modest in clothing and being comfortable too?"

"Yeah, that's right, and that should also extend to modesty in character as well," she said, "as Muslims, you're supposed to be kind, respectful, and well-mannered."

"Wow, that's deep, I didn't know that."

"That rule is for men too by the way," Anisa replied, "they're supposed to dress modestly and have good manners too!"

"I think it's beautiful the way you guys look trendy without wearing tight or revealing clothing," I smiled.

"Yep, I can still look classy and adhere to my faith you know," she laughed.

"I love the way you have unique identities without letting everything around you make you feel you have to dress and look a certain way. It must take some serious strength."

"That's the test of faith, babe."

"It's really refreshing the way you refuse to let all these billboards, magazine covers, and social media with hundreds of images of beautiful women who all look so impossibly perfect dictate how you look!"

Anisa shot a look at me.

"How come you're suddenly so interested, Riya?" she asked, "we've been friends for ages, you've hardly ever asked about my religion before."

"I've just been thinking about stuff, that's all," I replied plainly.

"You're right, it does take a lot of strength. Sometimes I do feel that these perfect looking women are laughing at me trying to cover up and be modest, but I don't care. For me the *hijab* is more than something I wear on my head; it's a state of mind: an awareness of God, awareness of my actions, being accountable, having a connection with Allah as you walk the streets embodying a symbol of Islam."

"That's deep, I didn't know you were so philosophical," I laughed. Something stirred inside me every time I learned something new about Islam. I don't know why and how, but I started to feel more spiritually aware, and I definitely wanted to know more.

It was the last Thursday of the month, which was when Dad got paid—that meant one thing for us: takeout night! It was also the only time that Dad didn't visit the local food bank or take items from the free community section of Mr Cooper's mini-market. We all sat by the kitchen table so we could hear him walk in. I was so hungry my stomach started to grumble. It wasn't too long until we heard his footsteps followed by the sound of keys as Dad opened the door to let himself in.

"Dad!" I yelled, "you're back!" My face lit up as I swung the door wide open.

Take-out night happened once a month. Dad allowed us to order whatever food we wanted. We usually ordered from Pizza Now, which was fifteen minutes' walk from our block. They had good deals on Thursday nights and the pizzas were slightly cheaper if we collected them.

"So you guys decided what pizza we're having today?" asked Dad, as he slowly took off his jacket and unclipped his tie. "I know what I'm having."

"Can we change it up a bit from our usual large stuffed crust meat feast this time?" asked Mum, looking through the colourful pizza flyer. "I fancy some chicken and black olives on our pizza."

"I'm sticking to my usual medium pizza, Dad," I said as I picked up the phone to make the order.

"Yeah sure, we can change it up a bit and I guess the boys will have their own two smaller pizzas since they'll never share with anyone." Dad scanned his eyes over the pizza flyer one last time. "Alright Riya, make the orders and we'll go and pick them up."

Take-out nights were the best! We hardly ever got to have fast food, so it was always such a treat. Dad and I walked to the pizza place and carried them back. They got cold very quickly and needed warming again, but I didn't mind doing that. I just wanted to zone out; zone out of our problems, zone out of life and live in a bubble, just for a few minutes. Take-out nights helped me do that.

We all sat on the living room floor and huddled up together facing each other. Those were the only times we sat together as a family to have dinner—Mum always said that was important, but we couldn't really do it because Dad was out of the house so much. I cherished those moments; I wanted them to last forever.

I watched everyone helping themselves to mouthfuls of garlic bread and pizza. The boys had their eyes glued to the TV as they ate. Aakil picked out the meatballs from his pizza first and then went for the slices. Dad placed two slices of pizza on a plate for Mum and got her a glass of water before sitting next to her to eat. I looked at everyone; they looked so happy and peaceful.

As the night ended, I watched Dad tuck Mum into bed. He made sure she took her medications and had a glass of water beside her bed. Looking out of the window I saw the clear night sky with only the crescent moon hanging like a jewel in the sky and a few stars twinkling in the distance. I looked back towards Mum and Dad's bedroom and it was at that moment that I realised that maybe Mum wouldn't make it. Maybe I had to start thinking about adapting to life without her. It was a thought I put off for so long, but the night's peaceful moment brought me to a realisation that no matter how hard I tried, I could still get an outcome in life that I didn't want. I didn't control everything, I couldn't. But that wouldn't make me stop trying for Mum. I wanted to keep at it, keep on doing what I needed to do; fight on. I had to. I worked so hard and I wasn't prepared to give up now.

Then I remembered Anisa's words again:

"Pray to God, He will listen."

Maybe I couldn't control everything in life, but surely there was a God up there that could control things. The more I thought about it, the more my faith and reliance on God grew. Raising my hands to the sky, I felt the volcano in my chest was about to erupt. I burst out crying:

"Oh God, whoever you are," I pleaded, "please don't let my Mum die, you know she's a good woman and a kind mother. Please don't take her away from us, please let us enjoy seeing her for many, many more years. Please, I beg you, please cure my Mum and let her stay with us!"

I wiped my tears away and put my head down onto my pillow. I couldn't help the hot tears from running down my cheeks and onto my pink pillowcase. The pillow slowly got soaked, so I turned it over and turned myself around to face my window. I gazed at the crescent moon again, which I could faintly see behind my net curtains until I closed my eyes and slowly dozed off.

Chapter 12

Mum

I woke up in a daze in the middle of the night to hear loud sounds coming from inside our flat. My eyes were half-open and my head was heavy. I forced open my eyes and looked around.

The muddled noises were getting louder as I slowly walked out of my bedroom, rubbing my eyes. I pushed open the living room door to find Dad panting and trying not to cry, but the boys went crazy, letting out loud sobs. Two large paramedics in dark green uniforms were towering over Mum.

"What's going on, what's happened to Mum?" I screamed, running my hands through my hair. My lips were quivering and hot tears were welling up in my eyes. I took a deep breath and tried to keep calm, but it wasn't working; I was finding it difficult to breathe. I swallowed hard, grit my teeth, closed my eyes and breathed for a few seconds to stop myself from shaking. Dad was kneeling on the floor next to Mum.

"Dad!" I yelled. He was shaking, his eyes locked onto the paramedics who were carrying out their observations and giving oxygen to Mum. "Dad!" I shouted again as I gripped his shoulders and turned him to face me. "Dad, you need to get the boys out of here, let the paramedics do their job."

He blinked several times and swallowed hard. "OK, OK, fine. Come on boys, let's get you back into your rooms."

Mum's pale body lay still on the living room sofa like a limp fish. She was unconscious. Her lips looked dry and I saw the green veins popping out of the sides of her temples. She'd complained of swelling under her ribs and severe headaches for the last few days.

"Alright... blood pressure, fine, heart rate, OK, temperature is fine... but we need to wake her up and get her checked over by a doctor so we're going to have to take her in," said the larger of the two paramedics whilst looking at his watch and pressing a whole load of different buttons on the portable monitors.

I went to the boys' bedroom to check on them. Dad wasn't in any state to go to the hospital.

"Dad, what happened? Why didn't you call me?" I asked.

"Your mum," he replied, shaking, "she was fine when I put her to bed." His teeth were chattering and he was breathing very fast. "Then she got up saying she wasn't feeling right, so I helped her up and walked her to the living room, but when I went to the kitchen to get her some water, I came back and she was just lying there, unconscious."

"You should have called me, Dad," I said.

"I didn't know what to do," he whimpered, "so I grabbed the phone and dialled 999." He passed his hands over his head and rubbed his temples. He swallowed hard and looked at me searchingly. I knew it wouldn't be a good idea to send him to the hospital with Mum.

"Dad, I want you to stay at home with the boys. I'll go with Mum to the hospital," I told him.

"What do you mean?" he mumbled. "No, I need to go, I want to go, she needs me...." he muttered as he tried to control the flow of tears from his eyes. He wiped his face with his sleeve. "Are you sure, Riya? Are you sure you're gonna be okay?"

"Dad, I'll be fine. I'll call you." I took a deep breath and went back into the living room.

They lifted Mum onto a stretcher; there was still no movement from her. They strapped her in and carried her down four flights of stairs. I quickly got dressed and followed them. As we reached the ground floor and came out of the communal door, the cold breeze hit me in the face like a punch.

They carried Mum into the ambulance.

Inside, I noticed everything was neatly and mechanically organised. Everything was colour coded and clearly labelled. They put some extra leads onto Mum to monitor her heartbeat and continued to give her oxygen. The strong smell of disinfectant harassed my nose, reminding me of the school toilets. As the ambulance slowly drove away, there was still no change. Her eyes were closed and her body was floppy. I reached out to hold her hand, which was stone cold even though she was under layer upon layer of fleece blankets. I tried to be positive, but I felt a huge lump in my throat and started to feel nauseous; it almost made me sick. I had to put my hand over my mouth to stop the retching. *I'm not going to lose you Mum, not today,* I kept repeating to myself.

When we arrived at the hospital, the paramedics checked us into the A & E department and left us in a room right in front of the reception area. I peeped into the waiting area on my left to see how busy it was. All of the grey coloured metal waiting room chairs were taken, with some people standing and others sitting on the floor. People were there with all sorts of different problems; there was one guy who was bleeding from his nose—*he'd obviously been in some sort of fight.* The nurse gave him some tissue for his nose, as he sat there gritting his teeth and resting one side of his head on the pillar to his left. Another guy was sitting with one of his trouser legs cut open—he had an injury on his knee cap. He held on to his thigh and rocked backwards and forwards. A police officer stood towering over him. *It must be gang-related,* I thought.

There was another woman who was holding her stomach and crying. She was trying not to sob, but occasionally let one escape. She was constantly looking at the clock and reciting something under her breath—*maybe she was trying to say a prayer.* There were only two nurses and one doctor in the main waiting area. The rest of the nurses were in the emergency unit. A few minutes later, I saw the two nurses and the doctor rush to the entrance of the A & E Department as an ambulance brought in another patient who needed urgent care. This time it was a young boy, with a bandage around his head and covered with a red blanket; he wasn't conscious. They rushed him straight into the Intensive Care Unit.

Mum obviously wasn't a priority in their eyes so they placed us in a separate room and left us waiting for hours. I walked out of our room and looked through the glass window at the entrance of the children's A & E unit, which was cordoned off from the adult's area. The area looked more pleasant with lots of toys, paintings on the walls, a colourful seating area and cartoons playing on the small

TV screen, but it was no better than the adults' A & E. I couldn't hear the children because of the soundproof glass, but everywhere I looked there were distressed children, some were crying, others were sitting on their parents' laps and some walked around in frenzy. I shuddered. It felt like I was watching an upsetting silent horror movie.

As I walked back trying to find my way, I noticed a prayer room beside the children's A & E department. I was curious; I wanted to see what it was like in there so I walked towards it. I approached the door, peeped my head around and walked in. I looked around the small room; the walls were empty and plain, there were a few beautifully designed prayer mats on the floor embroidered in different colour threads, and a few books stacked on the shelf by the window with the script of a different language on their spine. I took a deep breath, inhaling the sweet scent in the air. For some reason, I felt at peace inside the room and temporarily forgot all of my troubles and worries. As I took a few more steps, my legs felt heavy and my heart trembled. I could feel the tears gathering, blurring my vision. I fell to my knees and looked up towards the sky to say a prayer for Mum.

"Please, God, I know you're up there," I cried. "Please let everything be OK, let me take Mum home."

I wiped my tears and looked around. The room was completely still and empty. I stepped back out to return to Mum, feeling lighter than I did moments before.

As I hurried back, I was surprised to see a familiar face; Nadim was standing by the Reception area, fiddling with his phone. He looked around like he was waiting for someone, but he didn't notice me. His hand was on his thick pushed back hair as he held it off his face, his eyes still glued to his phone. I watched him for a few seconds, trying to read his face until our eyes met. I tried to look away, pretending that I wasn't looking at him, but it didn't work. He'd already seen me. He stood there staring right at me, forcing me to make eye contact with him. I could have just turned around and walked away, but I didn't. I wanted to talk to him. Luckily, he walked straight up to me.

"What you are doing here, Riya?" he asked in his usual mild-mannered tone. There was no way of making out his mood or feelings from those words even though I desperately tried. Seeing him there immediately made me feel nervous. My palms were sweating and I became slightly light-headed. I just smiled at him politely. For a moment I forgot that I was there with my Mum waiting for the doctors to see us. I didn't say anything, I just stared into those wide eyes of his and tried not to lose myself inside them. After a few seconds, he looked at me in a peculiar way. "Riya, are you OK?" he asked in a slightly sterner voice. I broke out of my trance.

"Hi, yes, Nadim, I'm fine. I'm here with my Mum, waiting for the doctors to see us," I replied quickly.

"Sorry to hear that," he said, "I hope she's OK." His tone was slow and measured. "I'm waiting for my friend, Musa—he's started a new job here as a hospital porter." He looked around again. "His shift finishes soon."

I didn't want to go into Mum's condition and why she was here.

"Ah, right," I said. I lowered my eyes to the ground, not knowing what to say.

"Riya, she'll be fine *inshallah*. Don't worry."

I nodded, trying to stifle my tears. We barely knew each other, but he always had this way of understanding what I was feeling without me even saying anything.

"I heard you've been selling cookies, Riya," he said, quickly changing the subject. "I haven't had a chance to try one, but I'm sure they're delicious!" He winked at me and smiled again.

I edged closer to him. He didn't even flinch. I felt his breath on the top of my hair as I looked up at him. "I'm only doing it for my Mum," I whispered, "it's a long story, trust me. I've got Tooth Fairy Syed and Stacy Roberts sniffing around at school and don't even get me started on Mr Phillips, he's got me worried too with that announcement in assembly the other day—God knows what he's planning." Nadim listened carefully and attentively. I felt his eyes constantly move to and from my lips to my eyes. I was hoping that maybe he could somehow help me or give me some advice about how to continue. I don't know why I found it so easy to talk to him, but I did, especially when there was no one around.

Nadim closed his eyes and let out a deep sigh. "Be careful with Syed and Stacy, those two bullies can make your life difficult. Stay clear of them, especially Syed!"

My eyes opened wider and I looked at him as fear gripped my heart. "What do you mean?" I asked, "I've heard he gets up to no good outside of school, but you don't think he'll try and harm me, do you?"

"I don't know," he replied, "just be careful with him—I've seen him hanging around with people who get up to all sorts."

I looked at him and gulped.

"My older brother got mixed up with dodgy people a couple of years ago, that didn't end well!" he continued. He sighed and shook his head before continuing. "Gangs in every estate are a nasty bunch—all of them!"

"There has to be something I can do," I told him.

"Syed is really friendly with some gangs outside school—you don't want to get mixed up with that lot!"

I didn't know how to respond. Fear shot through my veins.

"Why don't you change tactics and try selling on-line?" he suggested. "I mean turn your ingredients into easy to bake instant cookie packs and sell them online. Pack them nicely into small boxes, put a few fancy labels on them and I'm sure they'll sell like hot cakes. That way you could move away from selling inside school and stay off everyone's radar."

"I guess I can try that, but it sounds like a lot of work—I haven't got the time or the energy for that right now. Anyway, why does Mr Phillips want to control sixth formers selling stuff in school? Surely they need to focus on stopping students selling vaping sticks around the school." I looked at Nadim as he listened, nodding.

An alert ping went off on Nadim's phone.

"That's Musa. I have to go, Riya," he said, "see you soon."

I watched Nadim as he paced back towards the Reception area, slipping his phone into his back pocket. Just before he went through the double blue doors and into the foyer where the lifts were, he turned around, smiled and waved at me. I waved back with a smile, pressing my lips against each other. I stood there for a while watching the double doors flap until I couldn't see him anymore.

I thought long and hard about what Nadim said about how dangerous those thugs from different estates could be. But I had more urgent things to worry about. I cast my thoughts aside and tried to focus on Mum.

A doctor finally did come to see Mum about two hours later. She placed some sniffing thing under Mum's nose, which appeared to irritate her and wake her up. It worked—Mum was awake, and suddenly sat up, but she was very disorientated. She looked at me in a panic and then at the doctor. Realising that she was in a hospital, she slumped herself back down onto the bed.

"I understand you are undergoing chemotherapy and immunotherapy, Mrs Kaur, which is great and I'm sure they explained that these types of treatments have side effects," explained the Doctor, scanning through her notes on a clipboard. "One of those side effects is loss of appetite. But when that happens, you must try to eat something even if you have to force yourself. It's better to eat small amounts frequently than have one big meal a day. Otherwise, your blood sugar levels will drop and you'll faint—that's what happened today I'm afraid."

"She is going to be alright, isn't she?" I asked, scanning the doctor's face, hoping to be able to read it, but she didn't give much away.

"Let's just keep an eye on her for now," explained the doctor. Her face was expressionless. "I'll check her over and send you on your way."

"I don't like what's happening to me," said Mum, looking up at me and breaking down into tears.

"I know, Mum," I replied, holding her to my chest, trying to stop myself from breaking down as well. I didn't want to do that in front of her. Mum was always strong for us and now I had to be strong for her.

They discharged her shortly afterwards and gave her some vitamin supplements to keep her strength up and her bones healthy.

I helped her get up and get dressed before taking her downstairs. On the taxi ride home, I looked at Mum when she wasn't looking at me. I wanted to reassure her, tell her that maybe there was a reason for all of this, that maybe it was a test from God to force us to think and ponder about life, but couldn't bring myself to say anything. Instead, I thought about how Mum was when we were all little. I remembered all the times she took me to school and came to the assemblies to watch me. In Year 6 she had watched me dance to Madonna's *Holiday*—we had a new teacher who was obsessed with Madonna. I caught her watching me from the audience, but I kept my eyes away from her because I knew her big round smile would give me the giggles.

I also remembered the time when I hurt my leg whilst playing netball in Year 5. The school called Mum to tell her that I'd been injured. She quickly came into the school and demanded to speak to Miss Riley, the teacher who was supervising netball practice after school. I had to calm her down and reassure her that it was my fault I cut my knee, otherwise I think she would have punched Miss Riley in the face!

Mum was always very protective of us, maybe a little overprotective. "It's because I miscarried twice before falling pregnant with you, Riya," she told me. "At one point I thought I wouldn't be able to have children, but then I was blessed with the three of you."

Something stirred inside me after that conversation with Nadim, but I didn't know what it was. Each time I tried to give it some thought, I was distracted by Mum's worn-out face and the shivering of her hands against my legs as she leaned against me. She was no longer the strong and confident Mum I saw growing up. Whatever she was, I didn't care. I just wanted to have her in my life for as long as possible.

Chapter 13

Strange Things

When I opened my eyes the next morning, my body was aching. I was too tired to go into college. Anisa came over that evening.

"I saw your message, hun," she said, breathing heavily, "I hope Aunty is okay."

"She's fine, Annie, she's resting—we had a long night."

"*Alhamdulillah*, that's good to hear. You guys are always in my prayers." She put her bag on the floor and sat on the chair by my desk.

"What did you say, Annie? That word, I mean?"

"You mean *Alhamdulillah*? Oh, it means all praises are due to Allah. We're supposed to say that when we hear good news, to give thanks to Him."

"Yeah, I sometimes hear you say these words in a different language—I'm so used to hearing you say them, but I never ask you what they actually mean."

"It's an Arabic word, Riya. Anyway, have you got any lip balm?" she asked, changing the subject. "This cold weather makes my lips dry and crusty."

"It's in that drawer." I pointed to the small cupboard on the left side of my desk.

"What's this, Riya? Where did you get this from?" Anisa was holding the book I borrowed from the library.

"I picked it up a few days ago," I replied, "I haven't finished it yet, give it here." I stretched out my hand to take it back.

"How come you're reading about Islam?" she asked, flicking through the pages. "You've never seemed interested before. The book looks good though!" She handed it back to me.

"Yes, it's an interesting read," I replied, placing the book back inside my drawer. "I'm on the Ramadan section."

"Yeah, Ramadan is going be tough this summer," Anisa remarked, "it's during exam time."

"The month of Ramadan is always an interesting one at school," I said, "it's beautiful how it temporarily transforms people. People who have feuds lay off each other, the school is so quiet and there are so many students and teachers praying wherever they can."

"Yep, that's what the holy month of Ramadan does," she laughed, "if only the effect lasted the rest of the year!"

"Fasting eighteen hours in that heat must be tough. I don't think I could do it. I guess that's also a test of faith, like you said!"

"Why don't you try?" she asked, "You can join us this year if you want, but nothing must pass your lips, not even water!"

"Yeah sure, why not? I'm sure my body could do with a detox. But I'll have to keep a secret bottle of water in my bag, just in case!"

We both burst out laughing.

"If you submit to Allah, you can do anything and He will always help you—even fasting all those hours. Anyway, I've gotta get back before it gets dark, otherwise

Mum will have a fit," said Anisa, buttoning her light brown coat. She never stayed for long.

I always admired Anisa's commitment to her faith. I was definitely in awe of how she fasted those long hours last year in Ramadan without complaining!

Her final words kept ringing in my ear, "If you submit to Allah, you can do anything and He will always help you." It gave me the encouragement and belief that if I truly turned to God, He would come to my aid. Maybe then, He would answer my prayers and cure Mum!

The more I learned about Islam and saw how people practised it, the more I was drawn to it. It was like a strong magnet pulling me towards it. I didn't know how much longer I could resist its pull...

As soon as Anisa left, I remembered that I had a couple of local orders to deliver.

There were small drops of drizzle on that evening when things started to feel a little eerie. I came out of our tower block and got onto my bike ready to get my cookies to the customer. I didn't have to ride too far; luckily, they were both nearby.

As I cycled to my first destination, I went past a few hooded teenagers. There were always gangs roaming around different estates and getting up to all sorts of mischief. They went by different names depending on what estate they came from and usually hung around on the streets below the tower blocks. *I'd been riding for more than ten minutes, so they must be hoodlums from a nearby estate,* I thought to myself.

I rode my bike up the hill near Crescent Park and along the leafy suburban area of Hamilton Terrace for about fifteen minutes until I got into a small neighbourhood. I handed over the cookies, collected the money and was about to ride off to my second destination, which was another ten minutes away near the Swiss Leisure Centre. Just then, I heard a rattling noise and the faint chatter of different voices.

I looked around, but couldn't see anyone. To my left, I saw a dark metallic grey coloured car with dark tinted windows. It was parked up, the lights were on at first, but quickly switched off as I focused my vision on it. The car waited there silently like a stealth cat. *Who was that?*

I had a hunch someone was watching me, maybe even following me, but after a few seconds I shook my head and cycled on. I thought I was just being paranoid, but then, there it was again. A strange rattling noise. I stopped and looked back, but it was too dark and the street lights were very dim. I thought I could see the silhouette of a few boys on bikes, but couldn't be sure. I squinted my eyes to try to see clearly, but it was no good. It was starting to rain too, little droplets pelting the ground. I decided to continue riding and peddled faster.

As I peddled quickly, I heard the sound of at least one other bike behind me in the near distance—the bike peddles and chains sounded like metal chains hitting against each other. Every time I passed over a manhole, it sounded like someone was placing a lid over a hot saucepan. My heart started to slowly pound in my chest. My hands felt cold and my body shivered, but I grit my teeth and gripped the handle bars tighter, determined to carry on.

I looked back to see the dark grey coloured car in the far distance, just then, I heard it again—the rattling noise. Now I knew there was definitely someone following me. I slowed down and turned a corner sharply to see who it could be. I got off my bike and waited behind a white builder's van. But I couldn't see anyone, it was late in the evening and the soft raindrops weren't helping. I was late for my second order, so after a few minutes of waiting, I took a deep breath and continued to my location; a two-storey townhouse on the right side of the Swiss Leisure Centre. The noise from inside meant that some sort of party was going on. I didn't care, I just wanted to get home. I collected my payment and rode slowly towards the main traffic lights. The temporary stop messed up my journey plan so I had to plan a new route.

It was cold, damp and dark. I looked around, the streets were empty and the strange car was gone. It was time to go home. I cycled home as quickly as I could.

I had a pounding headache later that evening, so I went onto our outside balcony at the front of our block to get some fresh air. As soon as it hit 10 or 11 pm it was common to see groups of youngsters roaming around the estate like wild animals. Tonight, they were talking amongst each other and making hand gestures, but I was too far up to hear what they were saying.

A few minutes later I saw a car pull up. My heart stopped. It was the exact same dark metallic grey coloured car with dark tinted windows that was following me earlier! The rear side window came down and seemed to attract everyone like a magnet. I tried to make out what they were doing, but the tints and the dark interior of the car made it impossible to see anything. I had to get a closer look.

I climbed down a few stairs, to get to the balcony of the first floor. Things were a bit clearer, but the street wasn't well-lit and I still couldn't see who was inside the car. The parking spot was obviously carefully chosen; it was the darkest spot. As I looked closely, I could see a dark figure crouched forward in the driving seat. There was no movement, until the blue lights of a patrolling police car lit up the dim walls. The youngsters casually dispersed and the dark metallic grey car drove away, turning right to avoid the oncoming police car. Just then, for a split second, I saw the dark figure in the driver seat turn to the left to notice the police car. *Who is that? What is going on there?* My mind was buzzing; confusing thoughts and fears all fused together like mushy peas. I didn't want to be spotted so I hurried back inside.

Once I was back inside, I wanted to forget what I had just seen and go to sleep, but it was no use. My curiosity got the better of me, and I stuck my head out of my bedroom window and looked down. My window was on the side of our block so the view was very poor, but I could see the night-time "activities" start up again. Hooded youngsters at the bottom of the other tower blocks, quickly moving things from one person to another; some of them were on bikes, but most of them were on foot quickly walking from one place to another.

I thought long and hard about the strange noises I heard earlier when making the deliveries and that dark metallic grey coloured car. The more I thought about it, the more odd everything seemed. The only thing that did make sense was that I needed to keep up with my cookies so I could keep on helping Dad pay for Mum's treatment. That was my focus, my life's goal—to keep Mum alive for as long as I could.

I leaned back and sat on my bed. I closed my eyes, inhaling slowly.

I didn't cry very often—I couldn't. Not that I saw it as a weakness or anything, but at times I felt my tears had dried up. But at that moment, I couldn't help but let out a few tears when the bitter thought of losing Mum clouded my mind.

After a short pause, I opened my eyes to the roar of a car engine to see the metallic grey car driving past our estate for a second time. I was never outside at this time of the night so I didn't really know what was normal. It stopped near the tall iron gates, but away from the street lights. I was desperate to know who was inside that car. More importantly, *why was the person following me?* I took a deep breath, gritted my teeth and found the courage to do what I had to do.

Chapter 14

Dodgy Dealings

I had to find a way to get down there and get a closer look. Luckily Dad was on one of his night shifts, and Mum and the boys were fast asleep. I didn't want to wake anyone, so I tried to not make any noise as I changed into my black joggers, hooded jumper and dark trainers, before grabbing my keys and tiptoeing out of the front door. I headed straight for the stairs that ran through the middle of our block and made my way down. As I got to the first floor, I slowed down my pace and took a deep breath to slow down my breathing. I walked out of our block and closed the big new communal door, which the council fixed last week and put a fob key system on it for security; it felt solid. I flung my hood over my head, making sure that it also covered part of my face.

Gusts of wind threw cold air onto my face and almost took me off balance. I grabbed the bars of the bike stand in front of me, unlocked my bike and jumped on to help me blend in even more. I looked around. I couldn't see the grey car anymore, but there was a steady stream of hoodlums walking towards the gates of our estate. I rode my bike along the wall on my left, which our tower block overlooked and darkened with its shadow—it provided the perfect cover. As I reached the gates, I saw the grey car in the near distance—it was parked two blocks away inside the opposite estate waiting to be greeted by the usual suspects, who came in waves bigger than earlier. I suppose the dead calm of the night provided them with the perfect cover to conduct their dodgy dealings. There must have been at least twenty hooded youngsters standing around the car and making contact with the person in the rear passenger seat. Nobody spoke to each other. They hung around silently like robots waiting for instructions. One by one they would jump off their bikes and join an orderly queue. Every few minutes, four or five of them then approached the open window of the back seat, handed something to the strange figure and then walked away with a smaller package, which they tucked away inside the front part of their jeans or joggers. *The person in the back seat must be collecting money from these guys,* I thought to myself.

They went off only to be replaced by another group who joined the queue to hand stuff over—they were like silent bees flying around a beehive. As I cycled closer, with each push on my peddles, I felt my heart race faster. Reaching the grassy patch where the other bikes stood, I saw the driver again. I needed to get a closer look.

I wanted to see who was inside that car, in the back seat. I had to blend in with the boys, so I counted to three, laid down my bike and casually joined the steady stream of hooded individuals walking towards the car. No one noticed me. They didn't look left or right, they just continued to walk forward like zombies. I looked down at the ground and continued to walk towards the car, adjusting my hood to cover more of my face. Even the older ones who wore balaclavas and stood around the car on the lookout didn't notice me. I waited in the makeshift queue like all the others waiting to approach the rear car window, except I didn't have anything to hand over. The realization that someone could notice me dawned on me. I felt terrified but I couldn't leave the queue by that point because that would definitely alert everyone. I had to think quickly, on my toes. I knew that at some point, I would have to make a run for it, but when, I hadn't exactly decided. There were only six people in front of me, then three—my time was coming.

Reaching inside of the front part of my hoodie, I felt some money that was left over from the other day's takings. I couldn't count how much it was, but I could feel a few plastic bank notes between my fingers and thumb. I separated two notes from the small bunch and rolled them up like a thick pipe. My turn came. I approached the car window and put my hand inside like I saw the others do. I felt a big wide hand reach out and touch mine to take the cash from me. The cold skin and fingernails of a much bigger hand swallowed up my entire hand, pulling me forward until I let go of my grip. The money was taken from me, but I still felt the grip on my wrist. I moved my body forward, peering into the car, but I still couldn't see anything. With my face half-covered, I moved forward another few centimetres. I saw another hand shuffling inside trying to find a package to hand to me. A few moments later, I saw a small package making its way to my hand that was still in the grip of a mysterious individual. As soon as the package made its way into my hand, I felt the grip loosen and I had possession of my hand again. That was supposed to be it; I was supposed to be on my way like the other guys, except I wasn't one of them. I was here on a mission—a mission to find out who was in that car. I leaned forward one last time when, for that split second, our eyes met. With half of my face still covered by my hood, I blinked once and looked at him again. I recognised that face as he looked straight back at me. That dirty blonde hair and quiff at the front was very familiar. He wore a black jacket over a black top, but that didn't hide those familiar emerging wrinkles on his forehead or his big wide frog eyes. It was him! It was Mr Phillips! Mr Phillips—our new Head of Sixth Form. In that small millisecond, another gust of wind blasted at me exposing more of my face and strands of my hair, which fluttered in front of my eyes. I stared at him in disbelief as he stared back at me in terror.

"WHAT THE HELL!" shouted Mr Phillips. "GO, GO, GO."

I shot a glance at the driver who struggled to put the car into gear before sounding a loud horn and speeding off, the tyres screeching and skidding as it pulled out onto the main road. As the car sped off, its sudden movement made me trip and fall backwards onto the cold hard pavement. As I sat up, everyone looked at each other confused, trying to make sense of what just happened. Then their eyes fell on me—one by one, they all fixated their gaze on me. For a few seconds, I froze. My hood was down and my hair was still flapping in front of my face. I looked left and right to try and plan my escape route. I saw one boy take out his phone and flash his phone light towards me, the rest of them closing in on me like a hungry pack of wolves.

Looking up at them, my legs began to twitch and my feet trembled as I felt the cold, concrete floor against my palms. I looked at my bike, which lay on the ground a few metres away. I curled my hands into a fist. I wanted to leap off the ground and run to safety, but at that moment, it felt like my bones had no strength and my muscles were all out of power. I couldn't move!

Chapter 15

The Pursuit

Three of the tall hoodlums stepped forward. "Who is
that? What's going on?" asked a deeper, gruff voice.

As they started slowly walking towards me, I knew at
some point I'd have to move my body and do something
and not just sit there like a maimed animal of prey. With
only a few metres between me and them, the adrenaline
flooded my body, making me jerk. Just as my heart started to pound against my chest, I jumped up and ran towards my bike.

Reaching my bike, I grabbed it, jumped on and peddled as fast as I could. The sound of bikes and shouts of
"get her!" and "she can't get away!" were frighteningly
close behind me. I peddled harder.

The darkness dizzied and confused me. I couldn't
work out which way was home, but after a few seconds, I
saw the faint shapes and outlines of the new blocks that
were going up nearby, which I recognised. The familiar
sight calmed my nerves for what felt like a tiny millisecond, but the adrenaline made me go without stopping. I
continued to ride until I saw our tower block whilst the
aggressive voices behind me were getting closer. Then
it suddenly occurred to me; I couldn't go home—they'd
know exactly where I lived and that would put my family
in danger. I couldn't have that so I turned left out of my

planned route and onto another road, which was fairly quiet with only a few cars. I looked back. They weren't stopping. I rode in the opposite direction to my house in an effort to shake them off, but it wasn't working—they were getting closer. I slid onto Whitechapel Road, riding in and out of the leftover scaffolds from the market traders—that didn't work either; they did exactly the same and were still on my tail.

My heart beat frantically as I looked back to hear the jarring laughter of the thugs behind me. I could feel my lungs screaming, trying to keep up with the will of my muscles as I peddled harder. A sharp pain bolted from my ankle to knee, and then up to the back of my thighs, but I was in survival mode; I wasn't going to stop. My breath came out in small spurts, the cold air shocked my throat and lungs as I inhaled deeper, trying desperately not to give up. A tear trickled down my face as the mud from a small puddle smeared my trainers. The adrenaline wasn't enough to fight my fear and dread of what would happen if this gang caught up to me. There were too many of them; I wouldn't be able to fight them off, they could do whatever they wanted. I felt my heart and lungs pumping, but my body was giving up as I peddled forward. As the panic shot through my exhausted limbs, my mind was telling me I couldn't go on anymore. I was certain this was my end.

I looked up to see the sky transform into a dark smoky colour with small flashes of lightning that looked like faint human veins, followed by a deafening rumble of thunder. The rain spat out from the clouds like a barrage of arrows. As I came closer to Whitechapel train station, I went around the back of the station to try to lose them. Soaking wet, I peddled even faster, almost hitting a man who was trying to cross a small road behind the station. Then I spotted the staff entrance to the station—the door was open. I rode in, jumped off my bike and slowly closed the flimsy wooden door behind me. The dark green stained windows made it impossible to see out. I crouched down and peeped through the small keyhole to see the vicious-looking hooded thugs scanning their eyes around the station searching for me. They looked like lost children in a big supermarket.

After a short while, I opened the door only slightly and peeped through the gap. They were gone! I looked up to see the rain had cleared and the sky was a brilliant deep, dark blue. I took deep breaths to calm myself before jumping back onto my bike. I slowed down my pace and looked around every few minutes to see if I could notice anyone; luckily, the coast was clear. It was time to go home.

Chapter 16

What Just Happened?

I tiptoed inside and slumped on the living room sofa. The lights were turned off and everyone was asleep. I sat there thinking about what had just happened, what I just saw, and what could possibly have happened to me if they caught me.

I couldn't believe that I saw Mr Phillips right there in the middle of it all! How was he involved in all of this? With his posh privileged background that he never stopped going on about, I never in a million years expected to see him there.

There was only one possible explanation—he must have been making money from those street goons somehow. I wondered what he was placing into their hands... not that I could have done anything about it anyway. I had no proof, no evidence I could take to the police. *Who would believe that the head of my Sixth Form college was involved with street gangs?* It sounded laughable!

I jumped into bed and I tried to force myself to sleep, but the shock of the past hour kept me awake. *What just happened?* I tossed and turned in bed for hours trying to find a comfortable position. Every time I got settled in one position, that side of my body started to ache, so I turned over only for the pain to travel to the other side. The pain in my legs made it feel like they were pulling inwards. When I managed to close my eyes, it was only for little short bursts. I saw the most random things in my dreams; things I wasn't even thinking about. First, I saw Dad running to get to work on a cold rainy day, then I saw Mum walking me to school when I was little. I also saw myself arguing with Anisa about something I couldn't quite make out. Even the wildest dreams and discomforts didn't really bother me too much, but what did shock and scare me was a faint voice inside my head; an inner critic that constantly gave me a barrage of horrible, disordered thoughts, which I couldn't make any sense of. It felt like a dozen needles poking at the sides of my temples. It exhausted my mind and gave me a sharp headache. I didn't know what to make of it, I'd never experienced anything like that before. *What was happening to me, what was my body trying to tell me?*

The sound of my alarm clock instantly sent shockwaves through my body and made me jump up and sit on my bed. I was gasping for air, looking around my room like a mad person. Realising it was the weekend made me breathe easier. I lay back down and tried to close my eyes, but it didn't work. I barely got a wink of sleep the whole night and now it felt like the veins in my legs were pulling inwards. My mind turned into a whirlpool of scattered thoughts.

I couldn't fully digest what happened last night: blending in with the street goons; seeing Mr Phillips, then being chased by those vicious thugs. It all felt like a bad dream—I wish it was! I had a million different questions going around inside my head: *how and why did Mr Phillips get involved with those unsavoury characters and what would he do now that he knew that I knew about him?* Whatever the answers were, there was one thing for sure; I still had to continue selling cookies, whatever the risks.

I forced myself up and then slumped my head back onto my pillow again; I had a thumping headache. I didn't want to get out of bed.

I didn't usually drink coffee, but that was when I started. I needed a caffeine hit—it usually did the trick for Dad when he had early shifts and woke up looking like a walking corpse. I flung open the kitchen cupboard and grabbed the jar of the coffee Dad got from his last visit to the food bank. I threw in two spoons full into my mug, one and a half spoons of sugar, half a cup of boiling hot milk and levelled the remaining half of the cauldron that was my mug with boiling hot water to make my strong, sweet milky coffee. "Yuck!" was my response to the first sip, but then, very quickly, I started to like it, want it and need it every morning. It became a habit—a morning ritual before I went to college.

I spent the whole day in my pyjamas. I didn't want to do anything; I couldn't bring myself to even mix the cookie dough for Monday. I wanted to shake those feelings off; the feelings of fear and dread and get some fresh air, but I couldn't bear to go outside.

I sat in front of the TV mindlessly watching one programme after another until Anisa came over. I didn't want to tell her about the previous night. I didn't want her to feel I'd put her in any sort of danger from those thugs so I put on a fake smile, pretending everything was normal.

"What's going on down there?" I asked, standing at the window and pointing at the police van that was parked at the entrance to the Atlantic Estate opposite our tower.

"There was another gang fight last night from what I heard," she replied casually. I felt a lump in my throat and I swallowed hard. *It must have something to do with those thugs who chased me last night!*

"You say it like it's so normal."

"These fights are getting a bit too much—don't these guys have anything better to do?" Anisa shook her head.

"I wish those boys would just grow up," I said.

"It's not just boys, gangs in these estates have girls in them too, you know?"

"Well, I wish they'd just stop with all this gang rubbish." I let out a sigh.

"Anyway, you've been really quiet this weekend. You usually send a few dozen texts at least." Anisa looked at me and smiled before unbuttoning her coat. "Is everything alright?"

I wanted to tell Anisa about everything that happened the previous night, but I didn't want her to freak out and I definitely didn't want to put her in any danger. She was doing so much for me already and putting her neck on the line for me without even realising!

"I'm just worried about Mum," I lied as I turned around to avoid eye contact with her. "I hope we can continue with the cookies and carry on getting her treated."

"Well, why wouldn't we carry on, Riya?" she asked, her eyes following me as I placed her coat on the hook in the passage way. "We're doing fine with selling at school. Miss Alford is still letting you use her ovens and now you're getting a few outside orders."

"I know," I replied, biting onto my lip, "but what if someone creates obstacles for us?"

"Like who?" Anisa shot me a look.

"Like Mr Phillips for example!" I felt my throat drying up and my palms became damp at the sound of his name.

"Oh, don't worry about him, Riya," she replied, making a frown, "he's just being a busybody, probably aiming for his next promotion."

"Yeah, but what if he's not who we think he is, Anisa? What if he gets really nasty? I mean you heard his announcement the other day, what if he...?" I mumbled, thinking aloud. I felt the blood rush to my head. I placed my head in my hands, inhaling and then exhaling.

"Hey, where is this all coming from?" she asked, placing her hands on my shoulders.

I looked deep into her eyes and felt comforted by her warm smile. I wanted to tell her everything. It was at the tip of my tongue, but I couldn't find the words.

"Look, Riya. I know you're going through a lot, but all of this is a test from Allah. You know God sometimes tests us to make us better and stronger people," she told me.

I stared at Anisa's face, searching for answers. "I know, Anisa. It's just sometimes, I feel I'm not as strong as I thought I was," I explained, "sometimes I feel like I'm going to break."

Anisa grabbed my shoulders and shook me lightly. "No," she snapped, "you're not going to break. Allah will take care of you and always has your best interests at heart—you'll see that after this test passes *inshallah*."

"I know," I wiped my tears and swallowed.

"You are strong and tough," she added, "and the Riya I know has a lot more fight in her, OK?"

"Alright," I nodded. I closed my eyes, took a deep breath and slowly exhaled. I was beginning to feel Allah was watching over me and would always take care of me. I felt my hope and reliance on Him become stronger the more I read about Islam, learned something new from Anisa or contemplated life. I needed to gather more strength than ever now that I was facing another hurdle.

Anisa and I hung around for a short while flicking through the TV channels and enjoying the mixed fruit smoothies she bought for us. Her jokes and laughter made me briefly forget about all the worries on my mind, including what happened last night. But soon after she left, it dawned on me that I had to go into school and most probably face Mr Phillips.

I couldn't do anything with what I saw that night. I didn't have any proof so no one would believe me in school, not anyone important enough to do anything about it, anyway. I definitely couldn't go to the police—they'd probably fine me for wasting their time!

I have to find something, I told myself, *something I could use to go to the police. I can't just keep silent about what I saw!*

By the time Monday came around, I wanted to get on with baking my cookies—I had to, but I couldn't get myself out of bed. I sat up on my bed, looking around my room. Everything felt hazy like a dark tint of grey had been placed over my eyes. It was this darkness that started to chip away at my senses and replaced it with stomach-churning fear. The more I thought about Mr Phillips and what I saw a couple of nights ago, the more my fear grew. It tortured my guts, churning my stomach in tense cramps. It gobbled up my mind, knocking all other thoughts aside. I felt tired and overwhelmed from all the thinking, but I knew I couldn't stay in bed all day. I forced myself up, splashed some cold water on my face and got ready for school.

"Please Allah, protect me and give me strength," I muttered, grabbing whatever I could find in my creaking closet.

As I got to school, Anisa was already there waiting for me by the gates.

"I got your message, babe," she said, looking through her phone, "how come you decided to give the cookies a break for today?"

"It's OK, Anisa," I replied, "we're slightly ahead, we'll get back to it tomorrow."

"Sure."

I took a deep breath and tried to cast my fears aside as we walked through the school gates, but just as we walked past the main Reception area, I saw Tooth Fairy Syed standing by the new Sixth Form block. He stood there upright with his chest pushed forward and both hands behind his back like some kind of security guard. Stacy was there too, glued to his side, whispering something into his ear. He looked towards us with his cold dark eyes. I felt as if someone had poured petrol onto the small flame of fear in my belly that I was trying to put out.

"Look at him standing there like he's some sort of bouncer in a nightclub." Anisa rolled her eyes up and down at him. "Just look at those menacing eyes, I swear I can feel them all over us—what a creep!"

I didn't say anything and tried not to look at him as he was staring at us, looking hard with those big bulging eyes of his, creasing his forehead.

"Why is he gawking at us like that?" asked Anisa.

"I don't know," I replied, tugging at her to keep walking.

I tried not to show Syed that his presence bothered me. We walked straight past him and waited until we were out of his scope of vision.

Anisa and I separated as the pips sounded and I quickly made my way to my History lesson expecting to hand in my assignment to our teacher Mr Anderson, but he was nowhere to be seen.

"Your teacher is unwell today so I'll be covering," said a familiar robotic voice. I looked up. It was Mr Phillips!

My heart began to race—I could almost hear it pounding against my chest. I thought he was going to pick me out from the crowd and feed me to the sharks, but he didn't. He was his normal self—handing out the cover work, cracking a few jokes with the boys about last night's football game and then going around checking that everyone was on the right track. I tried to calm my nerves, but it wasn't working. As he came over to my table, I tried to act normal. I tried not to look straight at him. I kept my eyes fixed on my exercise book throughout our whole conversation. I smelt his strong aftershave and his warm coffee and tobacco breath as he crouched down to look at my work.

"Yeah, you seem to be on the right track, Riya," he said with his false confidence—I didn't expect him to know about A-Level History, it wasn't his subject. As he came a bit closer, I felt his warm breath on the back of my hair. "I know what you're up to," he whispered in my ear, his voice husky and coarse, "stay out of my way or you'll be finished in this school, do you understand?"

I didn't reply, I couldn't, I didn't know how to. *What did he mean?* I wanted to say something, but my vocal chords seemed to have stopped working. My hands began to sweat and tremble, which was starting to show; I couldn't even hold my pen properly.

I tried to hold myself together as I left the classroom. I felt Mr Phillips' eyes all over me, I didn't know what to make of his threat, I didn't know what he was capable of. I needed to do my own digging—I needed to find out more about Mr Phillips and make sense of what I saw on the weekend.

A few seconds after leaving his classroom, I looked back to see his eyes still following me, until Stacy walked in. He leaned over to speak to her, his eyes still locked onto me. I watched them muttering something to each other—I was too far to hear what they were talking about. As I turned a corner, I paused for a few seconds, turned around and peeped in. They were still talking and Mr Phillips looked around to see if anyone was watching, but they couldn't see me. He then handed her a small brown bag, but she shoved it back to him aggressively before storming out of the classroom. *What was that about,* I wondered, *was Stacy somehow part of his secret double life?*

Passing by the Reception area, I noticed Tooth Fairy Syed again. He was staring at me and followed me with his eyes. I saw him turn to look at Stacy in the distance. They both made me feel nervous, agitated. *Why was he looking at me like that? What did he want?* I tried not to feel scared of him—I didn't want to let him frighten me. I wanted to glare right back at him, but I couldn't. I didn't want to attract more unwanted attention so I looked away, pretending that I hadn't noticed him. He stood there, arms by his sides and hands in his pockets, upright like a brick wall. *He thought he was so tough!* But I wasn't going to be intimidated by him—not the way other people were. That's how he started on them; first the stare, then the casual pokes and prods to annoy the hell out of you. He picked on the younger kids first, then the girls—always in that order. Very rarely did he pick on someone his own age unless they were physically much smaller than him. Everyone knew he went to karate classes, so they probably thought he was a bit of a tough guy. Embracing his nickname and becoming Mr Phillips' pet must have made him feel like a real "hard man".

Seeing Syed and Stacy together got me thinking, what if they're both part of Mr Phillips' criminal schemes? I couldn't be sure, but since they were both Sixth Form Associates, they must be close to Mr Phillips, I thought to myself, they must be involved somehow.

As I walked out of the school building, something made me halt in my tracks. I turned around and looked back at the school gates. An idea popped into my head and I couldn't ignore it.

Chapter 17

More Confusion

I walked across the road and waited by the glass doors of the Stoke Youth Club right opposite our school. I waited until I saw Mr Phillips leave around about 5 o'clock. He walked out of the school clutching his briefcase and umbrella. My time came. I was desperate to find something I could take to the Principal or the police, I couldn't sit still after the way he threatened me!

I casually walked back into the school and past the Reception area, which was slowly emptying. The office staff were shutting their computer screens down and reaching for their coats and bags. I made sure no one was watching me and I went up to the second floor towards Mr Phillips' classroom and office. Some of the teachers were still in their rooms, I could hear their movements. I walked very slowly, almost tiptoeing until I reached his classroom and office space. It was made up of three brick walls with a thick frosted glass wall at the front with a frosted glass door on its right-hand side. It didn't strike me as a very secretive place where you could hide things. Hundreds of students passed by his room every day, not to mention everyone in his subject area who used the other classrooms on the second floor, but I wanted to have a look anyway—I had to start somewhere.

The cleaners usually left the classroom doors open during this time. I walked past them—they were too busy mopping the floors and wiping down the classroom tables to notice me. I let myself into Mr Phillips' space. I didn't have much time. I stood for a few seconds looking at his incredibly neat and tidy classroom. Every other class-room in the building looked like a bomb site, with piles of paper everywhere, student books in different piles sitting in different places, empty mugs in different corners and various documents pasted on every section of the walls. But Mr Phillips' room was very different; only a few items were stuck on his wall: his timetable and meetings rota for the week, allowing the cream and beige three-dimension-al patterned wallpaper near his desk to be clearly visible. His neatly arranged wooden desk sat in one corner of the room towards the back wall. It was huge, beautiful and had four posters the size of small tree trunks holding it up and a concealed back. *Where did he get the money for that from? All the teachers keep moaning that the school's budgets are very tight!* No one else had a desk like that. It looked a bit out of place, like one of those desks you would imagine in those posh offices in the city somewhere.

There was a dark brown leather mat on his desk with a bronze arched lamp shade to the left and a telephone to the right. His computer was on the centre of his desk next to a pile of papers to the right. Various piles of papers were neatly assorted onto a brown leather desk tidy and even his pens were neatly put inside the brown leather pen pot. The way his room was so neatly organised threw me a little bit; I didn't know where to start. I expected to come into a huge mess of documents, thinking I would have to rummage through the chaos to try to find some-thing I could use against him, but I didn't.

A thick small rug near his desk swallowed up parts of my shoe soles. It must have been hoovered very recently, because I couldn't find even a speck of rubbish on it. The only thing that was out of place was his half-empty coffee mug, which probably should have been cleaned—it sat on the shelf behind him where his coffee machine was. I lifted it to take in the strong aroma, which already filled the room.

My confused eyes scanned for a place to start. I went straight for his cupboards, which were empty except for a few transparent plastic folders, a small fan, some deodorant, a hair brush and aftershave. I went through all of his desk cupboards, opening and closing them one by one—they too, were empty, apart from a small newspaper cutting; a job advert for a new School Bursar—*why was he interested in that?*

Suddenly I heard muffled voices, which started to become louder. *Who was approaching, who could that be?* It was coming from right outside Mr Phillips' classroom, but I didn't recognise the voices. My heart started to race. As I heard the door handle move, I quickly ran around to the back of Mr Phillip's desk and crouched down. I felt my heart thumping and placed my hand over my mouth to silence my heavy breathing. I peeped over to see the door opening.

"This room is already clean and tidy," said one voice.

"Yeah, we can skip this one for today," said another.

It was only the cleaners doing their usual rounds—phew! They closed the door and left. When I couldn't hear their footsteps anymore, I reached for the filing cabinet beside the desk and looked through every drawer, which was neatly ordered with different files, each labelled and carefully placed inside: Sixth Form Assembly notes, Behaviour Reports, Attendance Figures, Parental Information, Medical Conditions—*all pretty routine stuff,* I thought.

Exhausted, I slouched on Mr Phillips' chair by his desk. There was no point. I couldn't find anything. I left in a hurry to get home, before someone else could spot me.

Chapter 18

Home: My Sanctuary

I came home to find Mum waiting for me. "I've run the water already, Riya, just mix it up for me with the bath salt." A strong smell of disinfectant from the bleach shot up my nose and made me retch as I walked into the bathroom. I poured Mum's vanilla extract bath salt into the hot water, trying to drown out the sharp bleach smell. Mum loved having hot baths, lying in the bath for at least an hour each time. She'd bathe in water that was way too hot for my liking, but in her current state it would make her feel very weak and nauseous so I mixed it up making sure that the temperature was just right.

"It's almost ready, Mum." I dipped my finger into the water to check the temperature; it was perfect. I moved my right hand back and forth inside the water to create bubbles like she used to do for me when I was a lot younger. With the bathroom steaming, the water was at the correct level and the smell of vanilla filled the entire room. I got a glass of cold apple juice for her in case she felt dehydrated in the bath. I turned around as Mum walked in and struggled to get undressed behind the cloudy smoke. I knew Mum didn't like anyone helping her with something as basic as washing herself so I tried to make the experience as pleasant as possible, by making sure that she felt relaxed and at the same time giving her privacy where possible. She was a proud and confident woman, so I tried to do very little to give her a sense of dignity and self-respect.

"Don't worry, darling, I can manage," she said, accidentally knocking her elbow against the shower guard and trying not to slip as she pulled off her top and threw it to the ground.

After a few minutes of shuffling about, still with my back turned, I heard Mum placing her bathrobe on the hook of the door and climb in. As she got halfway in, I turned to help her ease into a comfortable position. I poured the warm water on her back and arms and then wiped her face. She reached for her drink, which I guided to her lips, allowing her to take gentle sips as she lay with her eyes closed, soaking in the silky soft soapy water. I saw her taking in and enjoying the aroma of the vanilla scent. I enjoyed sitting beside her and looking at her so relaxed. It made me forget how ill she was and how much pain she was going through.

"We're really proud of you, darling," she said looking up at me, her lips trembling. "Mummy loves you so much, all of you."

"I know, Mum," I replied, feeling the soft skin of her arms on the palm of my left hand.

After a while, I helped her gently scrub her arms, her neck and her back. Finally, I washed her hair, which was becoming increasingly thin with patches missing—it looked strange, but Mum wouldn't shave it off. "This cancer has taken away and changed so much of me," she said. "I have to fight back and win at least some battles."

I attached the bath seat to the middle of the tub and turned my back to her again while she sat and finished washing the rest of her body. She then sat on the edge with her back to me and waited for me to cover her with her robe and put a towel over her head. With her one hand on the sink beside the bath and the other hand on my shoulder, I felt her entire weight on me as she lifted herself out of the bath. Clinging onto my arm, I helped her to her room and moisturised her face, arms and legs leaving her to finish off the rest of her body while I prepared her meal. I came back to dry her hair, which didn't take long at all.

"Mum," I said, brushing her hair, "I've been reading about Islam, as part of one of my assignments at college. I think it's such a beautiful religion."

"Make sure you focus on your studies, darling," she replied. "Yes, it's an interesting religion," she continued, "I used to have a few Muslim friends when I was working at the nursery before you guys were born. It's a shame that I've lost contact with those ladies." Mum handed me her hair lotion. "Just massage in a little bit please, darling, not too much." She let out a deep sigh. "I'm worried about your Dad, he's gone really quiet."

"I know, Mum. I guess he's trying to cope with everything the best he can really."

"I know, baby. I know it's happening to me, but it can't be easy for any of you. He was never like this—your Dad, I mean. When I first met him, he was a very confident man, who dressed really nicely and always took care of his appearance." Mum looked at their wedding picture on her table and smiled. "He had charm and a sense of humour, which he used to get out of even the most serious of situations. But I guess life's troubles, especially the last few years, must have taken a toll on him... not having a place to call home for so long and then dealing with my illness the first time."

"I know, Mum, but you're both strong... you'll get through this like you did the last time *inshallah*."

"What did you say?" she asked. She shot me a mild frown.

"I said you'll get through it."

"No," she interrupted, "you said *in-sha-allah*. I remember those friends of mine used to say that all the time. Why did you say it, Riya?"

"Anisa always says it, it must have stayed in my mind," I answered quickly. She gave me a peculiar stare before putting the cap back on the hair lotion.

She let out another sigh and continued talking about Dad. "I think now that it has come around again, your Dad feels defeated. He doesn't seem to have the 'fire' in his belly to fight anymore like he did the first time. Either that or he's preparing himself to let me go." She let out a small stifled cry.

"Stop it, Mum!" I cried, "You're not going to die, OK? No one is preparing to let you go, no one!" I held her to my chest and stroked her head. It was on the tip of my tongue—I wanted to say more, tell her about my interest in Islam, give her some reassurance that this is a test from Allah and that I had a firm belief that everything was going to be OK, but I didn't know how to say it. I was confident that she would listen to me—listen to what I had to say before making a judgement. She was a much better listener than Dad, but I just couldn't get the words to roll off my tongue. "I'll be back with your food, Mum."

I prepared Mum's meals with a lot of thought and care. She couldn't eat certain types of foods and there were other things that she needed to eat, but didn't like. I mixed things up and made something different for her every day: chicken salad one day; roasted vegetables with rice another day and salmon steak with a simple salad the next day. I got the fresh vegetables from Mr Cooper's mini-market opposite our estate—it was from the community section so I didn't have to pay anything. I then washed, prepared and cooked it myself with very little salt and a tiny bit of oil. I left Mum's food on her bedside table and went to check on the boys.

The boys ate anything I gave them—they weren't fussy. I usually gave them fish fingers or chicken nuggets with chips. After we finished, I kept some food for Dad and then put Mum to bed. Aakil and Aahan didn't need me to put them to sleep anymore—they climbed into bed themselves and fell asleep. I always checked on them just before I went to bed myself.

I sat on my bed that evening racking my brains, thinking about how I'd continue selling cookies to pay for Mum's treatment now that Mr Phillips was on my case on top of having to deal with Syed and Stacy. *How would I sell my cookies without anyone realising,* I thought to myself, *it wasn't possible!* I had to be clearly visible in school if I was going to make any money, which I knew put me and Anisa at risk now that Mr Phillips and his two cronies were on everyone's back!

But I knew I couldn't just sit there and wait for something bad to happen. I kept thinking about how to piece together what I'd seen over the last few days. I had to do something, I had to find something I could use to go to the police and report Mr Phillips or at least take it to our Principal. He couldn't get away with leading a double life—one foot in school and another foot in the criminal world, it wasn't right! *There must be something I missed,* I told myself. I sat there replaying the events of the last two days in my head with no end or conclusion in sight.

I was still awake when Dad came in at midnight. I made my way to the kitchen to warm up his food for him. I saw less and less of Dad since he was putting in extra overtime. As I watched him sitting on the sofa, I desperately wanted to speak to him and ask for his advice. He didn't know anything about Mr Phillips, Tooth Fairy Syed or the thugs that chased me a few days ago. As far as he knew, the cookies were being sold and were bringing in a little bit of money to help pay for Mum's bills.

"Dad, I've warmed up your food, it's on the table." He took off his jacket and clip tie, lifted his plate of food and slumped onto the living room sofa. He stared mindlessly at the TV, watching the football game as he gulped his food down. He must have been really tired. I saw him drifting off a few times with his plate of food still in his lap, waking up only to the sound of the television with a look on his face like he'd lost something. Mum came out in her night gown to join him a little later. I watched them both silently staring at the TV.

Just then, I remembered that I hadn't finished reading my book, *An Illustrated Guide to Islam*, which I was eager to finish—I was already halfway through the next chapter on patience and gratitude. It taught me the beauty of having patience and faith in troubling times and part of that was to be grateful for every blessing in our lives. But with Mum and Dad both in the living room, I wanted to tell them about what I was reading, just to see what they'd say.

As usual, I didn't rehearse anything—it never comes out right even when I do, so I decided to drop small bits of information to see if they'd take the bait and probe me to open up a little more. I inhaled and then exhaled, pressing my lips against each other. I gripped my hands onto each other and tried not to bite too hard onto my lower lip. Then I cleared my throat and swallowed.

"Dad," I said, "I've been meaning to speak to you both about something, something really important. I've done a lot of research and a huge deal of soul searching."

"Not now, darling, I'm really shattered," he interrupted. They both looked at me. Dad continuously flicked his eyes, struggling to keep them open. "We'll pick this up another time, darling, my brain is shutting down."

He got up and left shortly after.

"Oh well, maybe another time then. Allah knows when it will be the best time," I said to myself, before realising that I was constantly thinking about Allah. I wasn't even using the generic term "God" to direct my reliance, but I was using the name Allah, the Arabic term I always heard Anisa use. It was that small change that helped me focus on getting closer to the One I was certain was always helping me.

I went to my bedroom and looked down from my window. I saw two police cars patrolling the streets, but apart from that, for the first time, the streets below our block were still and sombre. The wind pushed the leaves across the children's play area on my right like they were in a race. The swings moved slowly back and forth and the wind was howling. I saw the reflection of the moonlight on the children's slides making it seem as though a miniature moon was sitting there, waiting to slide downwards. It looked so peaceful and tranquil. I wanted to go down and sit there. It was the perfect time, not like the mornings when it was filled with the screams and laughter of young kids and the chatter of mums who came through the playground with their unusual looking pushchairs, having just dropped their children off to nursery or school. It would help clear my mind, but I knew it wasn't a good idea—it was too late and Mum and Dad were still awake.

With my brain overworked and my body exhausted, I raised my head upwards to the sky to say a little prayer:

Allah, please help, help me figure this out, whatever it is, so I can continue to help my Mum. I know you can hear me!

I was so tired that I didn't even want to get changed into my pyjamas. I didn't have the strength or the energy to mix the cookie dough for tomorrow morning. I had some left from the previous week that I didn't bake—I'd use that for tomorrow. We'd have fewer cookies to sell, but that was fine since we were ahead on Mum's bills anyway. I wanted to go to sleep. *I'll deal with tomorrow when tomorrow comes,* I told myself. As I closed my eyes, my head felt light and I felt myself sinking into my mattress.

Chapter 19

Power, Greed and Money

I woke up very early the next morning. I needed to get into school. I needed to find a way to search Mr Phillips' space again; there had to be something I missed. The cookies were on my mind, but I had to give the cookies a break again. *I'll take more after school orders today,* I told myself.

The sun was slowly rising and the dark clouds were clearing as I reached school; it was empty and silent as a graveyard. The school gates were open with cleaners busy mopping the floors and staircases again. The smell of bleach filled the staircase as I placed my hand on the stair rail that led to the second floor of the main school building where Mr Phillips' office and classroom were.

As I reached the second floor, I walked carefully across the wet floors of the long narrow corridor and peeped through every classroom. Apart from a handful of cleaners, no one else was there. I headed straight for Mr Phillips's classroom again, but just then, I heard the sound of loud hurried footsteps coming from inside. I heard two separate sets of footsteps, which became louder as I got closer. I hid behind one of the grey stone-coloured pillars. I started to feel the palpitations in my heart again and my breathing got faster. I placed one hand over my chest and the other over my mouth to calm myself.

Even though the door was closed, I could hear bodies shuffling around, but I couldn't see them and thankfully they didn't see me—I was screened by the pillar beside the classroom. I slowed down my breathing and then tiptoed towards the classroom door. I was now right outside, and I could hear muffled shouting. I leaned my ear towards the door, desperately wanting to know what was going on.

"I can't help you anymore, you understand," growled one voice, "she saw me clearly, she knows who I am!"

"We had a deal," demanded a different, deeper voice. "If you make things difficult for me, I'll tell the Principal, Mr Faulkner, how you pay for all your expensive stuff and what else you've been up to."

"If she breathes a word to anyone, we're all going down, you understand? I've got too much to lose!"

"If you couldn't handle the pressure, sir, you shouldn't have got my boys outside working for you!"

I tilted my head to the side and tiptoed to peer into the classroom from the side. From behind the pillar and through the clear small glass pane on top of the door, I saw who it was: Mr Phillips, banging his clenched fists on his desk, his slowly ageing face ugly with anger. Standing right in front of him was Tooth Fairy Syed.

"This can't be happening," Mr Phillips repeated.

"Chill out, yeah," said Syed, "she got away last time, but when the lads catch her this time, she'll definitely quieten down, trust me!"

"Let's hope we can get rid of her like we did with Mr Gorton," added Mr Phillips, "everything should be in place."

"Don't worry, I'll get my boys to give her a proper scare."

"Do whatever it takes!"

My heart sank. This confirmed it—Mr Phillips and Syed were working together and I bet Stacy had a big part in their criminal schemes too. And now I was their target.

"There is one more thing," muttered Syed. "I saw Stacy last night. She doesn't seem to be on board anymore. She's very sneaky, I don't trust her."

"I knew she would be a liability," growled Mr Phillips. "Find a way to take her out of the picture and make sure she keeps her mouth shut too!"

Syed nodded.

I tiptoed closer to the door and peered through to see them clearly.

"I'll get her before the walls close in on me," barked Mr Phillips, whilst pacing around his classroom. His eyes were glued to the floor in front of him.

I felt my palms sweating and my throat dried up. I needed to get out of there. I turned around and ran past the cleaners and down the stairs, almost slipping on the slowly drying wet floors. As I reached the bottom of the empty staircase, I kept looking up towards the second floor and around to see if Mr Phillips or Syed had seen me or if they were following me, but no one was around, the coast was clear. With my bag on my shoulder and my phone in my right hand, I flung open the double doors to exit the staircase only to walk straight into Stacy. I bounced backwards onto the stair rails, my bag fell on the floor and everything spilt out. My phone slapped the cold concrete tiles and fell apart—the battery, sim card and phone case went in different directions. I frantically knelt down to pick up my things and put my phone back together. For a few seconds, I forgot that Stacy was standing right there in front of me, all I could see was her black studded boots. I thought she was going to attack me again after our last encounter, but then, the most unusual thing happened—she knelt down on the floor to help me.

"I'll help you," she said in a broken voice, which was very different to the aggressive barks I heard the last time we encountered each other. I didn't understand, it seemed surreal, something was different about her, something had changed.

"I'm sorry about last time," she mumbled, wiping her tears. "I was only mad because that toff Phillips yelled at me for not being able to sell much after you came onto the scene."

I looked at her trembling face, but I didn't say anything.

"It's not just the baked goods," she continued, "Phillips also makes us sell..." she took a deep breath but didn't finish her sentence. "He keeps banging on about needing the money and told me if I didn't get my act together, he'd find a way to get rid of me," she whimpered. "I need the money from my baked goods, my Mum relies on it. But I don't wanna sell his other crap anymore!"

"What's he making you sell and why? Tell me what he's up to," I demanded. Stacy didn't answer, she seemed lost and fragile—not the dominant force that she seemed like when I saw her selling her goods in school. As we both crawled on the floor picking up the last few items, I couldn't help but feel slightly sorry for Stacy. She suddenly seemed weak and vulnerable.

"What is he doing in the middle of the night mixed up with those gangs outside of school?" I asked.

"I can't talk now," she said, trying to stop more tears from gushing out. "I'll tell you everything, but not here, not now. Someone might see us, especially that Syed boy—that's his pet." I sensed the frustration in her eyes. "Be careful, I know they're up to something," she whispered aggressively, looking around. "Just act normal and stay off their radar until we come up with a plan. You need to go, we can't be seen together."

I closed my eyes for a few seconds and took another deep breath and continued to walk, but before I could reach the lockers area, Mr Faulkner, our Principal shouted "stop!" and held out both hands. "Come with me please," he continued in a firm tone, ushering me to his office.

As I entered the room, I saw Mr Phillips there, sitting at the table in the middle of the room with his notes. I couldn't believe it. As Mr Faulkner turned to close the door, Mr Phillips let out a sly snigger. Mr Faulkner took a chair and sat down at the table.

"Quite frankly I'm surprised that a good student like you would get involved in something like this. I still can't believe it," he said, removing his glasses. "But rules are rules and I must follow procedure."

"Sir," I replied, looking straight at him, "what have I done, what am I being accused of?" I didn't understand. I tried to keep calm, I had no idea what he was talking about! "Sir!" I protested. "Can you please tell me what you think I've done wrong?"

"I wish I hadn't seen this," he muttered. He took out two slim vape sticks from a brown bag and placed them on the table in front of me. "I am ashamed, Riya, truly ashamed," he repeated. "Mr Phillips directed me to your locker after an anonymous tip-off!" I didn't know what to say. I just stared at them blankly. I recognized that brown bag from yesterday; that was the brown bag Mr Phillips handed to Stacy before she shoved it back to him! I knew what was happening: I was being set up. Phillips and Syed must have planted that bag in my flimsy locker.

"But Sir... I—" I took a deep breath, unable to finish my sentence. *He's lying!* I wanted to scream. Anger was tickling in my shins and travelled all the way up to my head. The blood was thumping in my veins; I couldn't contain it any longer.

"I'm sure you know that vaping is strictly prohibited in school," he continued, "we don't even know how harmful these things are yet."

"They're not mine, Sir," I screamed, interrupting him, "I'd never do something like this, this is a set-up!" I stood up from my chair. I wasn't calm anymore, I didn't even try to be calm—I had no calm left in me! I shot a look at Mr Phillips who was sitting there smirking.

"So you're saying they're not yours?" asked our Principal, Mr Faulkner, looking at me with a confused frown.

"No, Sir, that bag isn't mine, I've never seen it before in my life, I swear!" I took a deep breath and sat back down.

"I don't know what to think, Riya," he sighed, placing his glasses on the table. "This is a serious matter, which I'll need to investigate thoroughly."

"What do you mean?" interrupted Mr Phillips, "surely this is an exclusion—she's obviously been supplying and distributing them to other students."

"I don't think two vape pens are enough evidence to support that notion, Mr Phillips," replied the Principal, "but thank you for your input." He then turned to me again.

"Until I've had time to look into this, as an immediate consequence, I must ask you to hand over your Prefect badge. You will be stripped of all Prefect privileges for the time being," he added.

"Fine!" I took a deep breath, unclipped my prefect badge from my jacket and handed it over. I felt like one of those disgraced MPs you see on TV who had to resign because they did something foolish and immoral. Except I hadn't done anything wrong!

I watched Mr Phillips screw up his face as his confusion turned into fury.

"This is truly unfortunate, Riya," continued the Principal, "especially as it's so close to your final A-Level exams." He shook his head. By the time he went into a long speech about how "school is for learning" and "smoking and vaping is bad for your health", my brain switched off. I didn't have the energy or the strength to defend myself or to explain everything to him. I wanted to tell him that the main culprit who was actually double-dealing was sitting in the very room we were in, but I couldn't. I would just sound like a crazy person—I didn't have anything to prove it!

As the Principal was tidying his papers away, he quickly stepped out to deal with something else. I was by myself with only Mr Phillips in the room when his phone lit up; he left it facing up on the table next to his planner. He quickly reached for it to stop it from making loud vibrating sounds. As he grabbed his phone from the table, it tumbled from his hand, hit the ground and landed next to my feet. I leaned over to grab it and saw the text message:

"Boss, I need another batch—big buyer! Tooth Fairy."

He snatched the phone out of my hand, scratching me with his overgrown nails. He looked at me through the corner of his eyes, his face vile with fury. He then looked towards the Principal, who was still busy outside before finally fixing his eyes on me again. "Don't you dare," he growled, "you little busy-body, no one will believe you anymore anyway. I was hoping for a bigger punishment, but it looks like this Principal is weak!"

I looked at him and shook my head. I finally mustered up the courage to say something.

"You're not getting away with this," I snapped, gritting my teeth. "I'll find something to report you to the police with. I'm not going to shut my mouth and keep quiet while you use youngsters to line your pockets!"

"You're going to be very sorry for threatening me," he snorted, smirking.

"You should be ashamed of yourself—with your double life and dodgy dealings!"

The Principal returned and signed some papers before they both marched me out of the office. It was humiliating. It was the beginning of the day so everyone was slowly arriving at school. I saw people looking at me—most with their eyebrows raised whilst others had wicked smiles on their faces like scary witches. I don't know why; I never did anything bad to anyone in school so there was no reason for them to laugh at me. Maybe they were rival sellers who were jealous I was doing better than they were with my cookies. I tried not to let their weird looks bother me as I made my way to the first lesson.

I don't know how I got through the school day, but by the time the pips sounded to indicate the end of the school day, I let out a deep sigh. I quickly packed up my things, flung my bag over my shoulder and headed for the school gates.

I walked home that afternoon shaking my head in disgust. I couldn't believe Mr Phillips and Syed would go so low as to plant something in my locker to try and get me kicked out of school. As I got closer to home, I slowed down my pace. I could hear the chatter of small children who were heading home from school and the voices of mothers as they rushed around with both hands glued to their pushchairs. As I walked through the alleyway, which led to my estate, I looked back to check to see if anyone was following me—thankfully I didn't see anyone. I reached the front gates of the entrance to our estate and placed my hands on its rusty black metal rails. As I pulled open the right gate, I heard heavy footsteps and the rustle of leaves from the hedges behind me. I gulped and swallowed hard. I felt my palms sweating and my heart went from nought to a hundred in seconds. I slipped my phone into my bag and was just about to walk through the gates when I turned around to see three menacing faces glaring at me.

Chapter 20

Taken

They gagged my mouth and pulled a straw-like sack over my head. There were two people on either side of me, grabbing my arms and tying them behind.

Before I had any time to think, I felt something tighten around my wrists. My fingers went numb within seconds and I couldn't see anything clearly. The dark, shadowy figures dragged me into what felt like the back of some sort of van. I tried to scream and shout, but I couldn't let out a single sound. My mouth dried up and I felt a retching feeling in the pit of my stomach. Panic shot through my body like an electric shock! I tried to kick and frantically move around like a captured animal, to wriggle out of the hands of my captors, but it was no use; they were much stronger than I was. I heard the double doors close and with it, any bit of light that helped me see through the sack that was over my head. The two aggressive beasts pushed me to the floor and held me down. We were moving really slowly. I didn't know what to do or what to think so I threw a few kicks hoping they would land on someone.

After a few short seconds, I felt my voice return. "LET ME GO!" I screamed. "LET. ME. GO. NOW!"

"You can scream all you want, no one can hear you," said an unfamiliar frightening voice. "We're going somewhere really far, really quiet... you'll like it there," he continued in his intimidating tone. I wanted to break down and cry, but I didn't want to do that in front of them so I took a deep breath and tried to remain calm.

My head was repeatedly pushed onto the cold hard metal floor. I could feel the cold surface on my cheeks even through the bag that covered my face. They pressed my face down harder every time the vehicle turned or went over a bump.

"Please, I can't breathe," I gasped, "let me up."

"Shut up, we're almost there," barked the one whose knee was against my back.

My heart was pounding faster and I still couldn't breathe properly. I started to feel dizzy and my stomach churned like I was going to throw up. I turned my face to the other side to make way for the violent coughs that burst out of my chest and stomach. I retched a few times, but nothing came out.

"Alright, sit her up," yelled a voice from the front of the vehicle, "we don't want her to pass out."

After what seemed like forever, the vehicle came to a halt. They lifted me up and dragged me out. I moved my head left and right, but I still couldn't see anything properly. It smelt of damp moss, wet rain and flowers like a place we used to visit for Geography field trips in school. I moved my feet around to feel the soft wet muddy surface below my feet. *Where was I?* I thought to myself. *Where were they taking me?*

"Come on, keep moving," demanded a sharp voice.

The mud was sticking to my shoes and I heard crackling under my feet as the two bodies beside me pulled harder. I swallowed, still feeling the gag in my mouth. I heard insects flying around, buzzing around my ears, a

141

buzzing which stopped each time an insect landed on my face. Each time I shook my head, the flying creature would fly off and buzz around my head. I closed my mouth and held my lips tightly against each other to prevent them from flying into my mouth even though I still had a sack over my mouth. Something brushed against my head; something wet and soft—maybe a spider web or leaves from a tree, I didn't know. The sack became loose, so I looked down to notice the beginning of a tiny pathway as we trailed across the sloppy mud. After a few minutes, I noticed what looked like the silhouette of some sort of hut. Just before they pulled me in, I noticed a small window, a door, some sort of lock and then darkness as the door closed behind me. My body slapped onto the cold hard concrete floor as they threw me down; I heard the crackling of a fire and the sound of matches. The paralysing fear curled up inside me and clung to my heart before spreading through my body like icy liquid. It was like nothing I'd ever experienced before. My cold body suddenly felt hot and sweat started trickling down the back of my neck. I felt the throbbing of my own eyes against my face, the thumping of my heart against my chest and the ringing of silent screams in my ears. Through the veil of my sack, I saw what looked like flames. In the shadows, I saw a man squatting on the floor near the fire like a tamed beast.

What did they want? I asked myself. *What were they planning to do with me and how was I going to get out of this place?*

For a few moments, everything went dead silent. My head was filled with white noise. I kept telling myself that it wouldn't be too long before someone came for me, that I'd be home soon. But nothing happened. A strange smell of burning tobacco and other strong smells crept up my nose, making my throat feel dry. I needed a glass of water. I was tired, hungry and frightened. I desperately wanted this nightmare to end. I was prepared to give them whatever they asked for, I just wanted to go home and be with my family again; just to be surrounded by their presence. I sat myself up trying to make sense of it all.

They finally removed the sack that was covering my face and pulled off my gag. I screamed as loud as I could, my voice piercing the air like an arrow and echoing inside the room as it bounced off the walls. I turned to notice the long square-shaped window—it was boarded up and the door next to it was closed. I scanned the door and watched the tiny bit of light that was creeping in through the small crevice underneath. The smell of burning wood disturbed my eyes and the hard cold floor gave me shivers.

"No one can hear you in the middle of these woods," said the bulky dark figure by the lit fire in the middle of the room as he stood up and slowly walked towards me. His dark eerie eyes locked onto me the whole time. A tangy damp stink came from his jacket as he shuffled me around, untied my hands and then tied my right hand to a pipe using some sort of hard tape. I looked at my left hand—it had lost some of its colour. I stretched it out and shook it until I felt the stiffness disappear and some of the sensation return. I looked at the cold hard concrete floor where they forced me to sit and felt the wet rusty pipe that my right hand was tied to. I pulled at my right hand, but it was no use—the hard sticky tape was digging into my wrists and showed no sign of loosening. I tried to poke at it with my other hand, but it was too stiff, and my hands were cold, so I gave up.

The room looked empty, the lit fire in the middle of the room was my only source of light, but it didn't make me feel any warmer. I looked at the door again. It was closed, but I could hear noises outside. The smoke from the fire oozed out of the broken corners of the boarded-up window.

The other dark figures hovered around me like predators looking down at their prey. Their faces were covered with balaclavas, which made their eyes look even more menacing.

"I knew we'd get you eventually," said one voice as I struggled to try to make myself comfortable. He picked up a spider from the window ledge and threw it towards me. I quickly pulled my legs in and squealed as it darted past me.

"What do you want from me?" I whimpered.

"WE don't want anything at the moment. But our boss wants a word. He said you've been sticking your nose into his business."

As the fire burned brighter, I looked around the room again and noticed piles of brown boxes that were stacked on one side.

"Welcome to our little storage warehouse," said one of the boys as he walked towards me, sniggering. He stopped, held out his hand, pulled it back and then brought his hand swiftly downwards across my left cheek. The hard slap made my entire face sting. The stinging lasted for at least a minute as I tried to adjust my vision to look at him.

He clenched his fists and was about to go for another strike, when a voice shouted "Stop! Boss said he wants to give her a little scare, make her listen." I remembered the text message I saw on Mr Phillips' phone. He must have panicked and ordered this.

"Listen up," said the second guy, "we're gonna step outside for a smoke. Then we'll decide what to do with you when we get back." I didn't respond. I just looked at the four of them.

They walked off outside the room until I couldn't hear their footsteps anymore. The cold, the hunger and the fear finally set in and I couldn't help but cry when they left the room. I cried like I'd never cried before, letting out a stream of silent tears. I heard myself whimper. I didn't want them to hear me so I tried to lean my face against one shoulder to cover my mouth—it didn't work. I was lucky to get away from them the first time they chased me, but now they'd finally caught up with me. There was no way out.

Every few minutes, they banged at the door, barked like dogs and made howling wolf impressions to taunt me. It worked; the sudden banging always made me tremble. I was scared about what they might do to me; the fear of not knowing was terrifying. *I have to find a way to get out,* I kept telling myself. *But how?* I couldn't think clearly, my uneasy heart leapt into my throat and hammered against my chest. The terror stabbed at my heart and made my body tremble and shiver. Then it spiked, weighing me down with dread. My stomach cramped, I felt like I was going to throw up. I took small breaths and closed my eyes to calm myself, but it didn't work, all I could see were angry faces with bloodshot red eyes.

Suddenly, I heard a faint buzzing sound. It must have been my phone vibrating. I sat upright feeling hopeful before I realised that my bag lay against the door frame; it was too far, I couldn't reach it.

In the near distance, I heard the sound of a police siren and then hurried footsteps that faded away. I couldn't believe it. *They must have run away,* I told myself. This was my only chance to be found by anyone and get out of there. I screamed at the top of my lungs:

"HELP! GET ME OUT OF HERE!"

A few seconds passed and I screamed again, but it was no use; no one could hear me. The fire was fading and I was worried that I'd be stuck in a pitch-black room all by myself. I closed my eyes to try and find some peace. *Please get me out of here, please answer my prayers,* I repeated in my head.

It was so cold I could see trails of my breath in the air. There was no way to keep warm, and now the fire was slowly dwindling out. I didn't know what to do. I kept trying to imagine home, walking through the door, hugging Mum and crawling up in my own bed after a nice hot bath. In the corner of the room, I saw a small mouse scurrying around. I squealed. I hated rodents—just the thought of it sent shivers down my body making all my hairs stand up. Very quickly, my feelings of fear, sadness and anger turned into rage and a desire for revenge. *If I make it out of here alive, the first thing I'm going to do is go to the police,* I told myself.

My mind was busy projecting frightening images of Tooth Fairy Syed and Mr Phillips, when I almost dozed off. I was woken up suddenly with a loud bang on my door; they were probably taunting me again. I was hungry and the cold made my joints sore and achy. I heard my phone buzzing every few minutes. I began to sob at the thought of my Mum worrying why I hadn't come home yet, and having no way to get through to her. I didn't know how much time had passed. I tried to block things out of my mind by closing my eyes and taking deep slow breaths, but it wasn't helping; my head felt light and dizzy.

Just as I tried to keep my eyes closed to shut everything out, the loud banging on the door shook me like a frightened baby. This time the banging was louder and harder, following laughing and taunting screams. I peeped through one eye and looked at the door; the banging shook the door frame and my bag which was still leaning against it. It was almost tipping over, but then the banging stopped.

Just as I was about to breathe a sigh of relief, the banging started again; a continuous loud thudding like the slow beating of a big drum. I looked at my bag again as it tipped over frontwards spilling everything out onto the floor, including my phone!

I slid my tied hand right to the bottom of the pipe that it was tied to and tried to reach the phone with my other hand—it was no good; it was too far. I have to use my foot, I told myself, so I pulled my body down using my feet until I stretched my right foot to reach my mobile phone. I slowly dragged it closer and then kicked it with my heel towards my left hand, which was untied. The slow-burning fire was almost completely dead. I looked around and started to feel the floor around me, but I couldn't see or feel my mobile phone. I let out a deep sigh and searched desperately; it was no use—I didn't know where it was. I must have kicked it too hard! Then I heard it buzzing again. I looked around to see my mobile phone light up behind me close, to the thick pipe that my right hand was tied to. I picked it up and held it close to my face; 15 missed calls and the battery was almost dead. Only one thing to do—I quickly pressed the home button five times to send out an emergency message. I looked at the phone again:

EMERGENCY SOS MESSAGE SENT it read, before dying completely.

Now that my location has been sent, hopefully, someone will call for help, I thought. For the first time, my heart fluttered with hope.

I slipped the phone into my pocket and looked around again. I couldn't see much; it was too dark, apart from the thin ray of fading light that was coming from underneath the door. A million disordered confused thoughts passed through my mind. I didn't know what to make of them. I closed my eyes and drifted off.

Chapter 21

Face to Face

I didn't know how much time had passed, but it must have been a few hours at least because my stomach was grumbling and my hands and feet were frozen by the time I woke up. Maybe they were going to leave me here forever, maybe no one was ever going to find me, maybe my kidnappers weren't even coming back.

Then I heard rustling and pulling at the door and then a huge kick, but it didn't open. A few seconds later, I heard what sounded like something was being shoved into one of the sides of the door, a cranking sound followed. Someone was trying to get in and it couldn't have been those street boys—*surely they had keys.* All of a sudden, a gust of wind hit my face as the door was yanked open. I saw two tall figures blocking out the slowly fading light that was behind them.

"Riya, thank God you're alright." Anisa fell to the floor and held me tightly. "We got here as quickly as we could."

"I told you she'd be here, the message you got from her just confirmed it." Stacy held the door open and kept a look out. She dropped the garden shovel that she was holding to one side. "Hurry up, we haven't got long— they'll be back soon."

"Are you OK, did they hurt you?" asked Anisa tugging at my arm, but she couldn't get the hard tape off. She took out her keys and began to poke small holes into the part of the tape that was between my wrist and the pipe that it was taped to. After a few seconds, my hands were loose.

I slowly got up and stood upright. The blood rushed to my head and it started to spin. I felt dizzy, almost losing my balance. Anisa held me against her tightly again.

"Where did they go?" I asked Anisa, my throat hoarse and dry like I'd forgotten how to speak.

"They're always out and about at this time doing other jobs," interrupted Stacy, "but I'm sure they'll send someone to check on you real soon."

"Anisa, how long has it been?" I asked, looking outside. The daylight had completely disappeared. "I lost track of time, how long was I gone?"

"It's early in the evening, you've been missing for a few hours, babe!" Anisa pulled at me. "Come on, let's get out of here!"

"Thanks, Stacy," I said, rubbing my wrists; they were still hurting. She nodded to acknowledge me.

"Where are we, what is this place?"

"We're in that foresty part behind Crescent Park. It's hidden, nobody comes here," she replied. "They use this hut-like thing as a warehouse," she explained, looking at the piles of brown boxes. "I don't know where they get it from or who makes this stuff for them, but this is where Mr Phillips and Syed keep their stock of vape pens and liquids."

I looked around to see rows of brown boxes stacked one on top of the other. I had so many unanswered questions running around inside my head, but now wasn't the time to ask them. All I wanted to do was get myself out of that place.

I let out a deep sigh of relief, but before I could run to the door, I heard rustled footsteps approaching. I froze and looked at Anisa, who looked back at me biting her nails and trembling. Stacy looked at the both of us and then towards the door, breathing heavily. The footsteps got heavier and the sounds of different voices were getting louder. My mouth dried up and my heart started to beat really fast. I ran back to Anisa and held onto her arm tightly. The hefty footsteps were just outside the door. Stacy ran to the door and jammed it with the shovel to stop it from opening. There was aggressive jerking followed by deafening thumps, which suddenly stopped. A continuous banging then started like a barrage of fireworks exploding. Finally, the shovel dropped and the door swung open, blowing a gust of cold air onto all of us. The three tall bulky looking thugs who snatched me earlier appeared from the darkness behind the broken door. Syed emerged from behind them and marched towards us with his chest pushed forward. He looked at me and Anisa with his creased forehead and hawk-like eyes before locking his beady eyes onto Stacy.

"So you think you can come into our ends and be the hero now, yeah?" he said, smirking. "I always knew you'd let us down!"

"All I wanted to do was sell my baked stuff and make a bit of money to help my mum out," she replied, "I never wanted to get involved with your stuff, you forced me!"

Anisa and I looked at each other, confused.

"I don't care what you have to say, little girl," replied Syed, his menacing eyes still staring hard at Stacy. "You've disrespected us—disrespected the East End Crows by turning on us!" He clenched his fists and gritted his teeth. "None of you are getting out of here until YOU learn to listen," he barked, pointing his finger and turning his snake eyes towards me.

"Let us go," demanded Anisa, "I've already called the police, they'll be here anytime now."

"You what?!" he growled like a beast, his smirk turning into a vicious frown. "You're gonna stay here until we're done. You see, Shams," he smirked, looking at one of his other goons, "I always said I'm good at making a profit; now we've got two new workers for the price of one!" He laughed hysterically.

"I'm not doing it anymore," screamed Stacy, "I'm sick of you and Phillips!"

I slowly started to walk backwards, thinking about how to get ourselves out of that place. The other three boys then slowly pulled out bats from under their clothes.

The cold, the fear, the hunger, the terror in their eyes; everything started to work through my body again. I froze up, I couldn't move, I started shaking again. I wanted to cry, I wanted to scream for help, but I couldn't do anything, I felt my brain lose connection with my whole body. Anisa squeezed my hand tighter.

In the far distance, I heard police sirens again. The three boys who stood behind Syed jerked back to look towards the open door—they heard it too. Simultaneously, they all looked at Syed and then ran, but Syed stayed, looking back to see his friends had left.

"Weaklings!" he shouted, turning around and shaking his head. "If you need something done, gotta do it yourself these days, can't rely on no one," he muttered to himself. He took out his phone and began to frantically dial on the keypad as the police sirens got louder.

"You're not gonna get away with this," said Stacy, "the police are coming for you and Mr Phillips."

"Shut up," he replied, walking up to her face with clenched fists. "This is all your fault," he growled, "all you had to do was help me shift more of my stuff."

"Never," she replied, "I've told you before—I'm not doing it anymore."

Syed's face turned red like a cherry. He gritted his teeth and clenched his fists tighter. Then, within a split second, he exploded into a fit of rage punching Stacy several times in the face and stomach, roaring like a hungry bear with each strike.

Anisa screamed and I closed my eyes trying to inhale my fear and quieten my heartbeat. I felt the adrenaline kick in as I watched Stacy tumble to the floor with both hands over her stomach. I wanted to help her, but my body froze. I looked at Anisa, she stood with one hand over her mouth and eyes locked onto Stacy. Syed stood watching over her, breathing heavily as she sat there touching her bloodied and bruised face. I couldn't help myself, after a few seconds all I saw was red. Fury almost completely overtook my senses. I looked down at the floor to notice the shovel Anisa and Stacy used to break into the shed. As Syed walked up to Stacy with his fists clenched, his back was turned to me. I slowly lifted up the shovel and walked towards him, almost tiptoeing. Anisa's eyes followed, with her jaw wide open. I lifted the shovel above my shoulders and swung it as hard as I could across Syed's back. He groaned in agony as he went crashing down onto the floor. His knees bent and he fell forwards, his face slapping the hard floor as it made contact.

I dropped the shovel and placed both of my hands over my mouth—I couldn't believe what I had just done! For a few seconds, I stood there looking at Syed as he rolled around the floor like a baby. He groaned in pain each time he tried to rub his back and neck. I was in a complete daze.

Chapter 22

Into the Darkness

Anisa grabbed me by the shoulders and shook me out of my temporary trance. "Riya, we need to go now!"

I swallowed hard and nodded. "OK," I told her, "alright, let's go."

We both turned to Stacy and helped her up. My hands were trembling as I rubbed Stacy's shoulders. Her face was bruised, and thick, maroon blood covered her grey top.

"I can't feel my face, Riya, please don't leave me!" Stacy started to shake vigorously. "I feel sick."

"You're going to be alright," Anisa told her, "we need to get you to a hospital, but first we need to get out of this hell hole."

Stacy looked at Syed, still struggling on the floor and moaning. "The police are coming for you, you big bully," she shouted.

We shot out of the hut like a speeding bullet into the darkness of the forest. Stacy closed the door and jammed it with the shovel.

"Follow me, I know the way," she said, wiping the blood off her face. She put one hand onto Anisa's shoulder and limped as she slowly led us through the dense forest and deeper into the blackness of the woods. I used my hands to claw through the tree branches as they constantly slapped my face.

Suddenly, Anisa screamed and started slapping all over her face and neck.

"Spiders!" she yelled, "They're everywhere."

"Let me see," I told her, taking a closer look at her face. "I can't see anything Anisa, I'm sure it's gone."

"Hurry up you two, we need to keep moving," yelled Stacy, looking back.

I felt pain everywhere in my body, especially my back and neck. I tried to shake it off and continue, but I didn't know how much longer I could keep going.

Just then, my left leg dropped into a big hole and I fell forwards into a bed of mushrooms; its fungus got all over my face and hands. A sharp pain cut across my eyes and head, I lifted my head and spat out, but the bitter taste of the mushrooms stayed in my mouth. I closed my mouth and tightened my lips, but it didn't help. I looked towards my leg and felt a ripping sensation in my ankle; the pain shot up my leg like a bolt of lightning. I couldn't move!

"Stacy, Stacy!" yelled Anisa, "Riya is hurt."

They both sat me up. I cried in pain.

"Stretch out your legs," said Anisa, "give it here, let's have a look."

I lifted up my jeans while Anisa beamed her phone light onto my ankle. It looked swollen like an aubergine. It throbbed and burned.

"I can't move," I cried, placing my hands over my mouth, "it hurts too much."

"Well, we can't stay here!" Stacy tugged at me, Anisa propped me up from the one side by putting my arm over her shoulder. "We have to keep going," said Stacy, still pulling, "not too long now until we see a pathway."

I held onto Anisa tightly as I limped, putting most of my weight onto my good leg. The pain was real; my brain ached with the effort to keep my body moving and prevent my mouth from screaming. We kept going. I didn't look back, I tried to shut my mind off from the horror of what happened inside the hut which was still not too far behind us. We continued into the woods, off the main path and through the trees. We stumbled on different plants and twigs as the mud stuck to our feet like glue. Pushing aside the numerous branches from poking our eyes out, I touched my face; my skin was clammy despite the cold. There was no breeze; the air was thick with the smell of wet tree trunks, soaked leaves and damp flowers. My mind started to play games; I thought I saw the shadows and colours between the trees moving by themselves. I blinked several times and shook my head to break out of it. As we moved further into the woods, the darkness lightened until I saw a small pathway.

"There it is." Stacy pointed ahead. "Not long now."

As we carried on into the darkness of the woods, the pathway seemed to widen. It wasn't long until I saw the outline of Crescent Park, a few street lights and rows of boarded-up abandoned tower blocks. Just then, before we reached the end of the forest, I heard twigs snapping and crunching leaves. I looked around to see who it was, but I couldn't see anything until in the corner of a hedge, I saw a pulled match light a cigarette. I still couldn't see who it was, but as we moved further along the path, he came out and walked sideways. I looked ahead—there he was standing at the edge of the forest, just before the woods ended. It was that sinister figure from the hut—the one who was squatting by the fire. He pulled at his cigarette, which glowed like a candle and lit up part of his face, exposing his weary smirk. He held up a small knife but didn't say anything—the cigarette in his mouth reflected on the blade of the knife and made it glow every time he pulled at it.

"I've got orders to take her," he said, pointing at me.

"Let us go and we won't say anything about you," Anisa pleaded, "we promise!"

He moved closer, still pointing the knife at me.

"You two can go, but I want her," he grunted. For a few minutes, we stood there; our eyes locked onto each other.

"There's no point," shouted Anisa, "the police are coming, you're all gonna go down!"

I looked at the unearthly figure again as he looked left and right. It wasn't long before he flicked his cigarette to one side and ran towards the abandoned blocks like a panther, disappearing into the darkened pathway.

As we continued and reached the end of the woods, I heard the blaring sirens of a police car followed by a sudden screech of tyres. Reflections of the flashing blue lights lit up parts of the forest that was now behind us, two police officers burst out of the car.

"Are you girls alright?" asked the female officer, scanning us one by one.

"They're both badly hurt," cried Anisa, "please, help."

The second officer reached for his radio.

"Ambulance required, I repeat ambulance required, sending GPS location details now."

Both officers came closer to look at Stacy, shining the light at her face. They asked me to lift up my jeans and shone the light at my ankle too; it was still pounding like a heartbeat.

The paramedics finally arrived after a few minutes. Stacy looked very drowsy, her eyes were closing. Sitting in the ambulance, I watched the paramedics reach into their green bags as they tended to me and Stacy.

I rubbed my eyes and slowly began to open them as they adjusted themselves to the brightness of the nearby dim street lamps. *I know this area*, I thought to myself. *It looks very familiar.* Then I remembered, we lived here once; it was one of the temporary accommodations the council placed us in a few years ago. *I wasn't too far from home.* The houses beside the row of sheds were empty and boarded up, ready to be demolished and replaced by posh-looking box flats like most of the old blocks in this area. It's strange how your brain can play tricks on you, making a familiar place seem suddenly very unfamiliar and scary.

It was dark and chilly. *Thank God everyone is fine,* I said to myself as I looked up at the sky and felt water on my face; cool drops of water. There was an enormous shaking clap of thunder as the rain fell, hammering the ground. The blue lights, the sirens, the fear of dying, the pain in my leg, seeing Stacy get beaten up—everything made me feel like something was cracking inside me, tears welled up in my eyes from the deepest depths of my heart. I felt I'd been spat out from the mouth of hell.

I looked at Stacy. She looked broken but she found the strength to smile at me through her bloodied face. With Anisa by our side, the ambulance silently drove off with its flashing blue lights, which lit up the dark empty streets. The police car followed us from behind.

Chapter 23

The Shake-Up

The ambulance stopped at the front of St. Christopher's Hospital. The paramedics walked us in and put me and Stacy into two different cubicles. It wasn't long until I saw Mum and Dad burst in. I limped towards them as fast as I could and ran into their open arms. Aakil and Aahan emerged from behind them and tugged at my legs as I grabbed hold of Mum and Dad as tightly as I could. My heart erupted and hot tears of joy rolled down my cheeks.

"Thank God you're OK, darling," whimpered Dad, "thank God you're not seriously hurt."

I looked up at Mum. Tears rolled down her trembling face as she silently stroked my hair.

"We'll have to take a full statement from you at some point, Riya," said a mechanical voice behind me. The police officer took out her pen and notepad and took some notes. "You get some rest now, we'll be in touch in the morning—while everything is still fresh in your mind."

"OK, officer, thank you," replied Dad.

"There will be two uniformed officers outside, for your safety," reassured the officer.

I stumbled onto the hospital bed and dimmed the lights, dragging my left leg.

I felt numb. My mind was blank except for images of that hut and the ferocious faces of Syed's goons, which

I saw every time I closed my eyes. Enough was enough, I was sure of my decision; I was going to tell the police everything—I wasn't going to hold back! Everything felt hazy, like I'd been away for such a long time. The faint lights still hurt my eyes and I felt tightness around my arms, hands and feet as if my skin was tightening and pulling inwards for some reason. *Maybe I'm just extremely tired.* I didn't want to talk anymore. I closed my eyes and dozed off within seconds.

I spent most of the night plagued by the most horrible nightmares that tortured my mind: the thugs who took me transformed into a sickening, revolting creature with glistening, black shiny skin and far-reaching tentacles—it looked like a big hairy spider. I saw myself trapped again in a dark cold room with a fire burning in the middle. I was tied up against the wall. My shoes were removed so I felt the damp, cold concrete floor. The smell of the burning wood from the fire went into my eyes and mouth until I could taste it. Behind the fire, I saw the creature with its eyes wide open and tentacles slowly poking at the fire, causing bits of the wood to fall on the floor—each time the creature poked the fire, a small bit of burning wood came closer and closer to my cold feet. I struggled to detach myself from the rope that was tied to my wrists and around my ankles. I heard the creature again rustling around and making hissing sounds. "I'm here," it said in its savage lowered voice, "I'm here for you." Then its voice changed. "We're gonna have some fun before the

Boss comes," it said in a sadistic tone. I didn't reply. I just watched as the creature moved from one side to the other still behind the fire, half exposed and half covered. Suddenly I saw it crouch down stealthily as if it was preparing to launch forward at me. My heart started beating fast and my palms were sweating. I wanted to get out, but I couldn't. After a few seconds of struggling to break free from the ropes, I gave up and stopped. I fixed my eyes onto the creature; it also fixed its eyes on me. Then before I could even twitch, it launched its entire body forward towards me. I gave the loudest scream I could, until I found myself in the hospital bed with my eyes wide open.

The sunlight was on my face, which strangely grew brighter and warmer. I wanted to wake up, but I couldn't, so I lay there with my eyes open. Then, as my mind played out the horrible events from the previous night, something really strange happened—something I've never experienced before. As I fought with myself to clear my mind, my palms and feet began to sweat and my body stiffened up. I felt my heart thumping in my chest. Suddenly, I felt my body jerk and jump forwards as if something was trying to come out of me. It all lasted for about five minutes until I managed to gather my strength and sit myself up. I put my hand to my forehead—I was burning up. My eyes felt sore and I still felt the aches and pains from the previous day; my back and elbow were bruised from when I was thrown on the floor, there were red marks around my wrists and my ankle was throbbing like a beating pulse. I didn't know if I was coming down with something or if I was feeling like this because of all the stresses and strains. Maybe it was a mixture of both.

In amongst that chaos of a million different disordered thoughts running around in my head, I started hearing that voice in my head again. Swimming amongst the waves of my chaotic mind like a water snake, I heard its faint whispers. I didn't know what it was. I hated feeling like this. In an instant, sadness took over my heart and I couldn't think clearly. *How was I going to help Mum like this?* I felt defeated and helpless. Mum just needed one or two more months to see if her treatment was having any impact. I was so close yet so far.

I looked around the empty hospital bedroom and took my phone off the charger socket to call Anisa, but I couldn't—every time I thought of Stacy my mind took me back to that hut, and I shuddered.

What happened that day peeled off the years of blind confidence that I had in my abilities. I used to think I was capable of anything—I kept telling myself that. But the reality was that no matter how confident I thought I was, I couldn't control everything. Some things were just way beyond my control, like those thugs who kidnapped me, Syed who probably wanted my blood and Mr Phillips who wanted to silence me in whatever way he could. Despite all of that, I still desperately wanted to fight my way through life and find my inner strength again, but after what happened, I felt like I didn't have any strength left in me. I was ready to give up; give up fighting, give up on my plans and give up on life.

I didn't know what I had to do to find myself again. I felt so many different things; I felt sad, I felt angry, I felt scared, and I felt bitter. All of it made me empty and unproductive, I didn't feel like doing anything—I just wanted to sit still quietly and watch the world go by. I was desperate to get out of this weird state, but I couldn't; as soon as I sat up on the hospital bed, it started again—I kept seeing those thugs from that hut and I kept hearing Mr Phillips' growling voice in my head. Just as I put my hands over my ears to shut it out, feelings of dread clung to my chest. I couldn't stop it; I couldn't control it. I needed to speak to someone, so I finally found the strength and called Anisa. I didn't know what she could do; maybe just give me some sort of reassurance.

"Hi Annie, it's me, Riya. Are you OK, how is Stacy?" I bit onto my lower lip trying to stop my slowly forming tears from gushing out.

"Riya, I'm fine—Stacy is recovering. The police drove me home after you fell asleep." Her voice was calm and soothing.

"Thank God," I sighed. "I've got a hundred different things going on in my mind and I can't see a way out." I started to mumble, I didn't know how to open up about the flashbacks and I didn't want to explain those weird sickening sensations in my stomach.

"What do you mean, Riya?" she asked.

"You know, with everything that happened yesterday. I keep thinking what if those thugs come back for me and do something worse!"

"You can't think like that, babe, the police are involved now. Hopefully they'll get Syed, catch up with Mr Phillips and put an end to this. You'll feel better then."

"This is not the first time I've encountered them," I added, "I should have gone to the police sooner."

"What do you mean?"

I told her the whole story about my run-in with Syed and Stacy, and the time I saw Mr Phillips on our estate and I got chased by his thugs. I also opened up about what I heard from Mr Phillips that day I went to look around his classroom. Then my mouth started to dry up again.

"Sounds like a complex situation. Mr Phillips must have a major part to play in this; he seems like a really nasty piece of work. Make sure you tell the police everything so you can put this whole thing behind you!"

"You don't think they're going to come after me, do you?" I interrupted.

"Who?"

"Those thugs—what if they hunt me down and really hurt me this time?"

"No, Riya, you can't think like that. The police will probably be in touch really shortly, just make sure you tell them EVERYTHING. I'm sure they'll follow it up and put an end to this entire thing and punish whoever needs to be punished."

"Are you sure, Annie? I mean what if the police don't get to them in time and they come after me?"

Anisa took a deep breath. "Riya, I think you're over-thinking all of this. Let the police deal with it now. You stay safe, be vigilant and if you ever feel like you're in any sort of danger, just dial 999."

"OK, Annie. As long you think so. Thank you."

"Do something to take your mind off things and get some rest."

As I hung up the phone on Anisa, I felt a bit stupid telling her about all the wild possibilities that were going through my head. I didn't want her to think that I was some sort of weirdo!

I placed the phone beside me on the bed and looked searchingly at the light blue hospital floor. I felt lost, I didn't know what to do with myself. Suddenly, the phone buzzed, making me jump—it was only a message from Dad telling me he was on his way to pick me up. I exhaled and closed my eyes.

A doctor arrived shortly after; the x-ray came back clear—nothing broken. They bandaged me up and discharged me with paracetamols and a crutch, but I couldn't leave without seeing Stacy.

I waddled around the A & E department balancing myself on my crutch and searched for Stacy. When I couldn't find her, my body went into panic mode again. I tried to control it by distracting my mind, but it was a constant battle. My mind started wandering again, projecting the worst possible scenarios about Stacy. My body started to feel stiff and the aches and pains returned. I slumped down onto one of the chairs in the Waiting Room and with my head in my palms, I let out a stifled cry. I was just about to give up when I looked up and noticed Stacy through the small window of the room opposite me.

I walked in to see Stacy lying flat on her bed. Her eyes were closed, her face was still swollen up and her right eye socket had turned black. There was a thick line of dried blood on her bottom lip, which was also cut and puffy.

Her mum was sitting by her bedside, holding onto her hand.

"I'm so sorry," I said to them both, shaking my head, "all of this is my fault!"

"No it ain't, dear," replied Stacy's mum, "it's my fault!" She was a well-built woman with broad shoulders, a round face and pale white skin that glowed as she tried to contain her tears.

I was confused. *What did she mean?*

"Ever since my partner left me, we've been struggling to cope," she continued, wiping away her silent tears. "I couldn't get a job cos of my disability and we were falling behind with the rent and bills."

"I'm sorry you had to go through that," I said.

"That's when Stacy came up with the idea of selling baked goods, but I don't know how she got mixed up with those thugs on our estate!"

Just then Stacy opened her eyes and let out a small groan as we helped her sit up.

"I'm so happy to see you well, Stacy." I kissed her on the forehead and sat down in front of her.

"Syed forced me to get involved, Mum," she said, "I had no idea Mr Phillips was behind it all until recently; I thought it was just Syed's thing. Turns out we were all at the bottom of the 'pecking order.'"

"Who's Mr Phillips?" Stacy's mum scratched her head.

"Never mind, Mum, long story."

"So what's his business in all of this?" I asked.

168

"I don't know that much, but that rotten thug Syed told me that Phillips is a gambler and owes a lot of money to different loan sharks."

"What, really?" My eyes lit up.

"Yeah Syed introduced him to his little gang and now they get some of the Sixth Formers to sell all kinds of vaping liquids in school and not just the legal fruit flavour ones," she added, raising her eyebrows.

"That's crazy, that stuff is lethal!" I couldn't believe what I was hearing.

"That's not all," she continued, "he's also been stealing money from the school accounts."

My jaw almost dropped to the floor.

"How did he have access to the school accounts?" I asked.

"He earned the new Principal's trust somehow I guess, but now that they're bringing in a new bursar, he needs to replace all the money that he took."

"That explains it," I said, "I saw a paper cutting for that job advert in his office!" I was stunned. Everything finally made sense.

Stacy ran her fingers across the bandaged stitches on her face. "Syed forced me to sell his stuff after I couldn't afford his extortionate fees," she said. "I know it was wrong and that's why I wanted out, but they wouldn't let me!" Stacy shook her head and exhaled. "I should have never got involved with those two!"

"The police are coming to see me today," I told her, "I'm going to tell them everything about Syed and Mr Phillips."

"Good. I'll tell them everything I know when they come to speak to me." Stacy grit her teeth before lying back down. She closed her eyes. "I hope they both get what's coming for them," she muttered. "I'm gonna try and get some shut-eye, these pain killers are kicking in again."

"I'm so glad you're OK, Stacy, I really am! Thank you for doing what you did."

Stacy nodded in acknowledgement before closing her eyes.

Before I had time to process what I'd just heard, my phone buzzed again. I took it out of my pocket:

I'm waiting for you downstairs, come quick!
Dad

Chapter 24

Disturbed Peace

I was hoping to nod off like a baby in my own bed after a night on that hard hospital mattress, but I couldn't put myself to sleep. As I lay in my bed with my eyes closed, my mind was busy thinking about everything that happened the previous day. The more I thought about it, the more my worries increased. I couldn't stop myself from creating negative possibilities for every single worry I had floating around inside my head. One thought gave birth to several other worries and those worries gave birth to even more wild and scary possibilities. It was as if my mind was a huge queen bee that kept creating other little bees that flew around inside my head, stinging me every chance they got. I kept on having these episodes—it started with one worry and then led to a million more!

As I tried really hard to stay out of my head, my heart started contracting and I broke out in sweats. My mouth became dry and I felt pain down the back of my legs, it was paralysing. Mr Phillips' grunting voice, being taken and held in that hut, running around in that dark forest, it all kept playing back in my mind like a horror movie—I could see, hear and feel how I felt on that night. I hated feeling like that, I wanted to cry, but I couldn't. It seemed like I didn't have control of my own body, like something had taken over.

I needed to get out; out of my head, I mean. It might help to speak to someone, but how could I explain to someone that I couldn't control my own mind? Anyone would think I'd completely lost my mind! I couldn't speak to Anisa, I didn't want her to think I was some sort of drama queen. Even if I did try to explain these weird sensations and thoughts to Anisa, I bet I'd break down in tears and get myself into a muddle without being able to make her understand. I didn't want her to think she had a weirdo for a best friend. These flashbacks started to frighten me, I'd never experienced them before and I didn't know how to cast the visions aside or the gut-wrenching feelings of fear that came with it. I thought I understood myself—I liked to think I knew how my body and brain worked, but I clearly didn't.

When I finally did fall asleep after tossing and turning for hours in bed, the most horrible dreams disturbed me all night. I saw different things all mixed together like dark shadows running around in the wilderness. I woke up in the morning gasping for air. *Where am I?* I asked myself. The beaming rays of sunlight hit me in the face, I couldn't even open my eyes. My heart was racing and my mouth felt dry. I looked around and reached for my water bottle, taking sips and rubbing my eyes before realising that I was at home, in my bedroom—I was safe, everything was fine!

DCI Huntley arrived along with two informed officers early the next morning to take my statement.

"I'm the investigating officer for this case," she said, after introducing herself.

Dad stayed with me throughout the whole thing. I felt very tense as I watched the two officers write down everything I said. I told them about Mum's illness and how I sold cookies to help Dad pay for Mum's treatment. I told them about Mr Phillips and Syed; the things I heard about them and what I saw them do. I also told them about what that gang of thugs did to me; the chase, the kidnapping, what I saw in the hut, and then the attack on poor Stacy.

"We've heard Stacy is fine and doing well," said DCI Huntley, looking through her notes in her black notepad. "Hopefully your swelling will go down too."

"We will look into everything you've said about Mr Phillips," she continued, "we take things like this very seriously. But we're stretched for resources at present so the wheels turn very slowly at the moment, but they do turn, I assure you!"

"Thank you," I replied, signing my statement.

"I am going to recommend you have some counselling, Riya. Someone from the Victim Support Unit will contact you soon," she added, "what you've experienced must have been very difficult for you."

I knew I needed some help, especially from the way I was feeling over the last couple of days. I needed someone to talk to, someone other than Anisa who I could completely open up to, someone who wouldn't judge me. I'd never experienced anything like this before. Maybe some counselling would help, but I didn't want to admit that in front of Dad—I didn't want to seem weak.

"OK, if you think it will help," I replied, trying to sound reluctant.

DCI Huntley and the two police officers left shortly after. Dad walked them out and left for work a little while later.

I noticed Mum sitting in her room by her small dressing table. I walked in to see if she was OK. She quickly turned away from me and wiped her eyes.

"Are you OK, Mum?" I tried to look at her face.

Mum didn't reply, she wiped her nose on her sleeve and took a deep breath.

"Mum," I whispered, "are you OK?"

"It's all my fault," she sobbed, "we should have never allowed you to sell cookies in school. It's my fault; all of it. Look what I've put you through!"

"No, Mum," I replied, "It's not your fault." I wiped my tears and gripped onto her trembling hands. "You didn't choose to get ill and it's no one's fault that Syed, Mr Phillips and those street thugs chose to do what they did!"

"What if something happened to you, baby?" she whimpered, "if we hadn't agreed to you selling..." Mum took a deep breath and exhaled slowly, struggling to control her sobs.

"No, Mum," I interrupted again, "I chose to help you and I don't regret what I did even though it landed me into a lot of trouble. If I had to do it again, I would!"

"I want you to stop with these stupid cookies now," she demanded, "no more!"

I didn't reply, I just held her tightly against me. Luckily, we were ahead with the payments for her treatment, so I wouldn't have to think about selling cookies for another week or so.

I'll worry about it when the time comes, I thought to myself.

I didn't go to school for the next two days. It was Thursday so I decided to take a couple of days off and have a long weekend—I needed it. I didn't do much—I just hung around at home looking after Mum. I didn't even go out. I didn't have the strength to face normal life. I was scared to go out after what happened.

I kept having flashbacks and remembering stuff. I remembered different smells: the damp smell of the woods outside the shed; the smell of thick smoke from the fire that was burning inside; and then the smell of clean sheets from the hospital bed. I felt cold—remembering the cold hard floor of the van and the concrete floor inside the hut. I kept touching my wrists remembering the hard plastic tape that they used to tie up my right hand to a metal pipe.

I tried to shake it off. I needed to get a grip, take control again, but for the first time in my life, I felt trapped and cornered. I wasn't usually like this, I knew what to do on most occasions, but this time I became numb.

By the time the weekend came, I withdrew into myself even more. Feelings of resentment began to slowly set in. I resented everything: our money problems; Mum's cancer; Syed and his thugs who wanted to hurt me; Mr Phillips; the hospital bills and my cookie-selling which had come to a halt. I spent most of my time in my room racking my brains and scribbling ideas onto various bits of paper about what I'd do to get back on track with everything; I still had exams to revise for and I needed to revamp my cookie-selling cycles. By the end of each day, there were bits of paper lying in every corner of my bedroom. I felt like a magpie trying to build a nest with white lined paper. I began by thinking up something—an idea, strategy or plan and then I hit a brick wall. My brain looked at it closely and exposed its faults, making me start again.

I felt the throbbing pain return to my leg, so I limped into the bathroom balancing with one hand against the towel rail, trying hard to stand properly. Just as I touched the cold taps, the nightmare visions of the hut flooded my mind. As I reached to open the bathroom cabinet above the sink, I noticed something strange; I looked at myself in the mirror, but I couldn't see properly, my eyes felt blurry. I opened the cabinet and grabbed paracetamols, but I couldn't read the big letters on the packet properly. I brought the blue packet closer to my face, it didn't help; everything was wavy and blurry. I swallowed hard and tried to take a deep breath.

What was happening to me? Am I going blind?

I looked at my face in the mirror again, I couldn't see anything, it was a huge blur! Suddenly, the deep snarling voices of the thugs who held me captive echoed in my ears. I started to feel strange and uneasy. I felt pins and needles everywhere, I couldn't move, like I was in some sort of trance, I felt trapped. A sharp headache cut through my temples and started to pound—a continuous throbbing on one side. It felt like the skin around my head was getting tighter and pulling inwards. My stomach churned, it made me feel sick; a sickness that was coming from the pit of my stomach. I started to retch, like I was going to throw up. I looked at myself in the mirror again, I still couldn't see properly. I felt my eyes water, I wanted

176

to cry, I wanted to scream but I couldn't. I held onto the taps to stop myself from losing balance and slowly sat myself onto the edge of the bath. I tried to sit still, but I couldn't—the aches and pains in my legs made me jump. I tried to take deep breaths to try and calm my nerves, but it didn't work. I felt my heartbeat increase and my breathing became more shallow and rapid. I felt trapped in my own body, there was nothing I could do, so I covered my ears, closed my eyes and slid onto the bathroom floor.

In the midst of all that chaos, I heard that voice again, but this time it was a lot louder and clearer:

"They're on to you," it said in its half-squealing, half-whispering voice. "They'll come for you again."

"Shut up, you don't know anything," I whispered loudly, covering my ears. *"You're not even real!"*

It continued for what felt like forever, then after a while, I felt exhausted, like I'd just come back from a long jog. My body boiled up and broke out into sweats. I felt my heartbeat slow down and my breathing started to feel a little slower. I stayed sitting on the bathroom floor. The whole episode lasted for about fifteen minutes, until my heart settled and I started to feel normal again.

By the time Anisa came over in the evening, my brain felt like it was going to explode; the negative thoughts, my body going into panic mode and the fear of what lay ahead when the police began their investigations was overwhelming. I decided I was going to tell Anisa how I'd been feeling.

"I've been having sleepless nights," I told her, "and I get these weird sensations in my body." I tried as best as I could to explain the feelings: the shortness of breath, the nauseous retching feeling from my stomach, the rapid heart rates; the aches and pains in my body and the wild scenarios in my mind. But I couldn't bring myself to tell her about the voice in my head, I didn't know what she'd think—it sounded crazy even to me!

"It sounds like you've been having panic attacks, Riya. It's probably from the shock of everything," she explained. "You need to get it seen to before it gets worse. My mum used to have them after that car accident a few years ago."

"How is she now?" I asked.

"A lot better now *alhamdulillah*."

"How did she get better?"

"She doesn't like talking about it much, but I remember she went to the GP and took a course of tablets and had some sort of counselling too."

"I don't know, Annie, do you think it will help?" I asked.

"I think so. You need a bit of support my darling, otherwise it could get much worse."

"OK," I nodded, wiping my tears, "I'll get some help."

"Here, try this." Anisa handed me her air pods, which I fixed into my ears.

"What is it?" I looked at her wearily.

"We all have worries and moments of panic, Riya, even me! But try not to let it get on top of you." She scrolled through her phone and paused. "Whenever I've got stuff playing on my mind and I can't sleep, I lose myself in this. Just a few minutes and it calms me down." She pressed play.

What I heard next, I can only describe as words that I didn't understand in a soothing melodic voice. The sounds, the echo, the obvious rhythmic tone was like nothing I'd ever heard before. For a moment, I was lost in tranquillity. It brought me to tears. I pulled both air pods out.

"What was that?" I asked, smiling and wiping my tears.

"It's a recitation of the Qur'an. How did you find it?"

"Beautiful," I replied, "not like anything I've ever heard before."

"Let me find it for you," she said, reaching for my phone. "It's all on Youtube in case you want to listen to it again." Anisa fiddled around with my phone until she found the right clip. "This isn't a permanent solution," she explained, "I still think you need to speak to some-one—this is just to soothe you when you find things are getting on top of you. I've added it to your playlist, take a deep breath and listen when you can."

"Thanks, Annie," I nodded, taking back my phone. "I definitely will."

Chapter 25

Things Change

I spent most of my time in my bedroom; I didn't want to be around anyone. But after a while I felt suffocated, I needed to get out, I needed some fresh air, even if that meant going downstairs and out of our block for a few minutes. I pulled on my joggers and my hooded top, slipped on my trainers and headed for the stairs.

As I reached downstairs, I opened the communal door and let myself out to feel the cold breeze on my face. I held the door open and enjoyed the fresh air, the smell of white roses that grew on the flowerbed beside the tower filled my nose. I looked beyond the children's play area to see a small abandoned bike, which lay on the ground, but before I could look past it, my mind raced back to that night when I was chased by those thugs. I wanted to go out, but the thought of being confronted by those thugs terrified me, so I decided to stay inside, in the small foyer area.

I paced around mindlessly. I felt lost inside. The foyer was a tiny bit of space, it was empty—exactly what I needed to gather my thoughts and clear my mind. I was an organised person, someone who normally had a plan for everything, but when things didn't go to plan, it usually threw me off balance, like now! This was definitely my lowest point!

I looked outside and noticed a few children on the green grass patch of the children's play area. The mild sunlight nourished the evenly cut green grass, which was still wet because of the morning dew. The swings, slides and playhouse were all empty and the concrete pathways leading to the two exits were clear of the usual sweet wrappings, plastic bottles and drink cans.

Just then, as I started to lose myself in my head, through the glass window of the big communal door, I thought I caught a glimpse of Nadim. I ran out, leaving my temporary place of security and was about to put up my hand and call him, but he must have seen me in the corner of his eye as he already stopped.

"The Cookie Dealer! Hey," he said, projecting his high smile and exposing those white tile-like perfectly straight teeth of his. He made me blush. Biting onto my bottom lip, I tried not to smile back, but I couldn't help it.

"Is that what people are calling me now?" His big bright wide eyes made me feel all giddy. He made me temporarily forget everything that I'd been through over the last few days.

"I've always called you that," he laughed, pushing his hair back into position as the wind threw it to one side. "Sorry to hear about what happened with your Prefect job," he continued, "don't worry, I'm not judging." I caught a glimpse of that dimple emerging from his smirk.

"I didn't do anything wrong, Nadim, I swear to God," I told him. "I was set up!"

For the first time, I told Nadim about my difficulties and everything that happened over the last few days. I couldn't help it—it all came out of my mouth like a waterfall.

"I'm really sorry, Riya, I had no idea," he said, pressing his lips together. "I'm glad you're OK and if you've told the police everything, you're going to have to wait it out and let them do their job. I know they're really slow." As he moved closer, I felt my blushing come on again so I dropped my eyes to the ground. He made my heart beat so fast again, I was fighting to stop it.

Anisa's voice echoed in my mind, "he's a good Muslim boy!" I took a step back—I didn't want him to feel uncomfortable in my presence. He was such a nice guy, so easy to talk to, such a gentleman. He seemed a bit surreal, but I guess there are plenty of good people in this world—Nadim was definitely one of them.

It helped—talking to him I mean, but I was careful in what I said to Nadim. I didn't open up to him about my weird episodes—I didn't want him to think I was crazy. Telling a fresh pair of ears that I was struggling (even if I didn't tell him everything), definitely made me feel a bit lighter. These conversations always ended like this; apart from the odd conversation here and there, we went back to being largely unknown to each other, even in college. These times where I felt close to him only existed for brief moments. I knew I liked Nadim, but I didn't know what those feelings meant. There was too much happening in my life to think about things clearly. Maybe he liked me too, or was I misreading his natural good manners and friendliness?

As I parted from Nadim, I saw an ambulance quickly approach our block. Two paramedics came out and made their way to the big communal door. I ran to let them in.

"Who are you here for?" I asked hurriedly.

"Mrs Kaur, second floor I think it is..." one of them replied.

My heart jumped up to my throat: Mum! I had only just left her! The two paramedics ran ahead of me, and I followed from behind. They stopped at my door and knocked repeatedly. Mum was by herself, there was no one to open the door. I ran towards them and took out my keys.

As we got in, I saw Mum lying on the living room floor face down with the house phone still in her hand. They rushed her to the hospital immediately, but not before my panic shot to the roof. I felt a seizing sensation inside my body like I was going to freeze. *Not you again*, I muttered to myself, *I can't do this now*. At the same time, the voice inside returned. "She's going to die, she's going to die, this is the end," it kept repeating in its slow, sly, wheezing voice.

These weird sensations and that torturous voice started to wear me down, it was exhausting. I was sick of fighting with my heart and my mind. At times I felt I couldn't control it. I couldn't stop it. I wanted to cry, I wanted to scream, I wanted to break everything around me. I clenched my hands, gritted my teeth and closed my eyes to try to regain control of my body. *Get a grip, Riya,* I told myself and tried to focus on Mum.

As the paramedics carried out their observations, I couldn't hold it in any longer; I burst out crying, I thought this was the end.

"Please, Allah, please no," I kept repeating in a chant under my breath.

"Her pulse is fine, so is her breathing," said one of the paramedics, "she's still unconscious and given her medical history we're going to have to take her in."

I couldn't utter a word; my mouth went dry. I closed my eyes and took short breaths, allowing what was happening to me to run its course. It was the most horrible feeling ever. I thought I was going to die, but I remembered what Anisa said about panic attacks. I closed my eyes and took more deep breaths, and after a few moments, I started to feel like my feet were back on the ground again. I looked up to see the paramedics place Mum onto a stretcher, ready to carry her out.

"I'm coming with you," I finally managed to say before following them out of our flat and into the ambulance.

By the time we got to the hospital, Mum looked very frail, her black eye sockets deepened further and she looked worn out, exhausted. She'd put on so much weight that her face was puffy and her hands and fingers looked swollen, which looked weird for her usually slim figure. She couldn't even stand properly. We were going to lose her. I just knew it. I sat by her, giving her sips of water to keep her hydrated whilst a nurse took blood samples. I kicked myself for leaving her by herself.

"I'm so sorry, Mum," I cried, bursting out into tears. I felt my heart squeezing into a tight ball. "I've let you down, Mum, I've failed you. I'm so sorry." I didn't know what else to do, I was sure she was going to die this time, but I wasn't ready to say goodbye.

About an hour later Dad arrived. He was wearing his work uniform; his name tag was still attached to his jumper. I sat him down and gave him some water. I tried to take control of the situation because I knew how Dad got when he stressed out about Mum. He must have been thinking the same thing; that these were Mum's last hours. He sat by the chair beside Mum's bed staring at her like a helpless child. He took sips of his water as tears rolled down his cheeks.

"She didn't look right when I left her in the morning." Dad wiped his eyes with his sleeves and ran his fingers through his hair. "I called as soon as I got a moment; your mum said she was feeling really nauseous and weak," he said. "I feared the worst and called the ambulance before making my way to the hospital."

"You did the right thing, Dad. It's my fault, I shouldn't have left her by herself."

As we waited for the results of her blood tests and other scans, I tried to think about Mum in her normal state. I took myself back to a happy, fond memory of when I was a child. I remembered Mum waiting for me outside my classroom when I was in Year Six well before it was time to go home. She'd be there with the dual buggy, laughing and joking with the other mums. She always looked radiant with a glow on her face. She looked beautiful. Even when Mum was upset, her facial features never changed. You could never read her face. She would literally have to tell you that she was upset, otherwise you couldn't tell. She always looked happy, even that time when she was upset with Dad for burning her favourite beige and floral maxi dress—he accidentally put the iron on the wrong setting. He meant well by trying to iron her dress for her, but it obviously didn't work out. I lost myself in those pleasant memories because that was the way I wanted to remember her: strong, confident, elegant and beautiful. It made the waiting less agonizing.

It wasn't long until a doctor arrived wearing his white coat and black spectacles. Dad and I were already in tears. I held onto Dad's hand and stared at Mum, trying to put on a smile under the flurry of tears. "Mr Kaur," said the doctor scanning through various graphs and holding them onto the light. "I have some good news and some bad news," he continued, rotating the various graphs and looking closely at them. "The bad news is that your wife will need to look at her diet again very carefully and we'll throw in various supplements for her to build up her strength again over time, but the good news is that we have compared our scans with the ones we took during her last outpatient appointment and it looks like the cancer is receding—I mean retreating backwards. The clinical research trial treatment you are undergoing at the Bellington Hospital seems to be working very well. I think another three months or so with that treatment and correct medications combined with an effective diet and we should hopefully see the cancer go back into remission."

Dad and I looked at each other puzzled. Our tears dried up from the confusion. "You mean, my wife's not going to die then, doctor?" asked Dad bluntly.

"No, Mr Kaur," said the doctor. "With the right changes, she's hopefully going to make a steady recovery."

Mum sat up on the hospital bed. She looked at Dad, then at me and then at the doctor, before going into a daze, but she didn't say anything.

I ran towards her and grabbed her as tightly as I could. Warm tears rolled down my cheeks.

"You're going to be OK, Mum," I whimpered, "everything is going to be fine."

Dad slumped down onto the bed beside Mum and held us both. He didn't ask anything else and neither did I. After a few seconds Dad stood up and kissed us both, wiping his steady stream of tears.

All this time, we were expecting to say goodbye to Mum and thought about how we would adapt to life without her and now we were being told we no longer had to do that; that Mum would be with us and we no longer had to say goodbye to her. I thought about all the things I could now enjoy with Mum after she'd made her recovery. I could go bike riding with her around Crescent Park again like we used to when I was small; we could go swimming together; she would be there during my exam results days, my graduation and maybe even my wedding! She would probably see her grandchildren too. The thoughts and the possibilities were endless.

Mum was discharged from the hospital later that afternoon.

I called Anisa as soon as I got home and told her.

"*Mashallah* that's great," she said, "I told you everything will be fine, you just need to have patience and do your best with difficulties in this life."

"Thanks, Annie," I told her, breathing a sigh of relief. I felt a bit lighter like I'd won a battle even though I knew I had so many other things to sort out in my life, but at least this one major problem was coming to an end.

"I'm so grateful, Annie, I feel really lucky," I told her.

"Good, you should," she replied, "make sure you do something to show your gratitude to Allah."

"Like what?" I asked.

"Give some money away to charity; to a worthy cause, like a children's charity," she said, "anything good that happens to us is from Allah's kindness and mercy."

"How can I show that I'm grateful?"

"The way we show that we are grateful is by recognising that Allah has been merciful to us and then by doing a good deed like helping those in need."

"Sounds very noble."

"That's what Islam is all about, Riya," she explained, "being grateful by showing kindness and generosity to those less fortunate than us."

I thought a lot about what Anisa said—about the kindness and generosity that Islam encourages to those less fortunate to show gratefulness to the Creator. It's something I'd never thought about. I was intrigued, eager to learn more so I stretched out to grab hold of my *Illustrated Guide to Islam*, which was sitting in my bedside cupboard. I finished reading the last few chapters that night, then finally made my decision. I knew what I had to do next.

Chapter 26

The Gruelling Sessions

My routine was all over the place throughout the few days I spent at home; I fell into a vicious cycle of sleeping late and waking up late. I lazed around until the early afternoon, but I tried to do different things to occupy my mind, to keep it distracted. I loved to read, but I couldn't read when I was worried because my head hurt so much. I needed to do something physical, maybe go for a walk, but I didn't want to go outside—quiet walking would just bring about more ridiculous thoughts. Trying to watch something on TV only worked for a few minutes. I found it hard to navigate around my crazy thoughts. This was always followed by that insidious voice in my head that was trying to taunt me. I could almost hear its snigger and muffled voice. I tried to block out its voice, but it didn't work:

"Look at you," it said. "You didn't do this for your mum, you did it cos you like it. You like acting bossy. You like ordering people around and you like the smell of money when you count your takings."

"Shut up," I demanded, knowing that I shouldn't be having a conversation with my own mind. Engaging in conversation only made it worse. It was as if my reply gave the voice a "new life"—something else to say and taunt me with. I knew that I had to ignore it, but I couldn't.

"Just look at you! Distributing your little cookies and making your friend sell them for you. Who do you think you are—some kind of big boss?" The voice then laughed hysterically—a continuous provocative and insulting laugh until I was able to find the strength to focus my mind on something else; something completely different.

I tried to control my breathing and focus my mind on something pleasant; a happy moment; a moment from my childhood. After about fifteen minutes, I started to feel normal again. I took a deep breath, splashed some cold water on my face and tried to get on with the day.

I can't go on like this, I told myself. *I really do need to get some help before this thing takes over!*

I walked into the kitchen to find a white envelope with my name on it sitting on the kitchen table. It was a letter from the Victim Support Unit. I quickly opened it and scanned it from top to bottom. The first counselling session was in a couple of days, but in preparation, I had to complete a questionnaire they sent over to me:

"Over the last 2 weeks, have you been bothered by any of the following problems? If yes, please give further details:

1. Feeling nervous, anxious or on edge?

2. Not being able to stop or control worrying?

3. Worrying too much about different things?

4. Trouble relaxing?

5. Being so restless that it is hard to sit still?

6. Becoming easily annoyed or irritable?

7. Feeling afraid as if something awful might happen?"

Typing up my answers was one of the most exhausting things I've had to do—it forced me to search deep within my heart and mind in order to explore my thoughts and feelings. In my answers, I included details about how I'd been feeling after being kidnapped: the intrusive negative thoughts; my physical symptoms of sweating; the aches and pains; difficulty breathing; the nightmares, and that voice that was troubling me so much! I felt so drained after completing the questionnaire that I was dreading the first face-to-face session. I took a deep breath and I emailed over my answers to the Victim Support Unit.

My mind was all over the place as I anxiously walked to my first counselling session. My counsellor Amanda invited me into one of the consulting rooms—it smelt of lavender and everything was neatly organised; from her desk which sat at one end of the room to the tissue box, water jug and cups that sat on the middle of the table. I sat opposite her on a soft, comfortable sofa and sipped my glass of water.

"Riya, I've read your answer to our questionnaire," she began, flicking through her notes, "is there anything else you want to add, change or elaborate on?"

"Not really," I said, "I could say more, but I'd be repeating myself to be honest." I kept biting my nails. I couldn't sit still.

"From what you've described in your questionnaire in a lot of detail, it looks like what you're suffering from is Post-Traumatic Stress Disorder (PTSD)," she explained casually. "It's common for people who have experienced the kind of trauma you've faced."

"I thought it was some kind of panic disorder," I replied, "I did Google my symptoms."

"Well, I don't recommend Googling any symptoms—it's not always accurate," she advised, smiling. "The panic attacks are the result of your PTSD, Riya."

"Why, why is it like this?" I asked, "Does this mean I'm going crazy?" I sipped my water and swallowed hard. "And what about that horrible voice I can hear in my head?"

"No, don't be silly, of course you're not going crazy," she said abruptly, "the good thing is that you've done the right thing by seeking professional help."

"I don't know where to start," I told her, "I can't talk to my parents about it, they wouldn't understand." I felt a tear roll down my cheek.

"I'm aware that some communities may not be well-equipped to address mental health concerns, but a lot has changed over the years—we might not be where we want to be, but most communities are much better informed nowadays," she replied.

"What are these horrible thoughts I keep getting and that nasty voice that keeps taunting me? It's like I can't even control my own mind." I started to tremble, but I tried not to get too emotional.

"You are not your mind," she explained, "you need to remember that. Automatic Negative Thoughts or ANTs as we call them are just a bluff; they send messages to your brain telling you that there is something to fear when actually you are not in any danger."

"What about the physical things I feel in my body?"

"Those are the physical symptoms of your anxiety which have been brought about by your trauma. First the ANTs will get you to catastrophise everything in your mind, then it will start to come out in your body—heavy

192

breathing, nausea, the aches and pains, which seem very overwhelming. Sound familiar?"

"How do I stop them," I asked, "I don't know what to do, who to call or who to speak to. I'm sure if I explain this to someone, they'd think I was a mad person."

"No, Riya, you can't think like that."

"That's why I haven't spoken to anyone about this properly. I just kept it inside hoping it would go away on its own."

"It's great that you've now decided to do something about it."

"What can I do?" I asked again, "How do I stop it?"

"As for the ANTs or negative thoughts, there are different ways to deal with them; some prefer to challenge them in order to expose why they are false. For example, you could list them on a piece of paper and for each one, write down why you think they are not accurate."

"That sounds useful," I replied, nodding my head.

"There is also another method, which I find to be very effective. I always tell my patients to treat them, the ANTs I mean, like snowflakes falling AROUND you and not ON you. That means when they come into your mind, simply ignore them—don't question them, challenge them or try to get rid of them. Just let them be and eventually, they will naturally go away. The more you challenge them, the more they'll grow and feel overbearing. That same thing applies for that 'voice' you think you can hear—we all have our own inner self-critic, the important thing is not to listen to it and get on with life. Ignore, ignore, ignore! I think you should start with this, it's called the Acceptance Method and see how you get on."

"What about the panic attacks?"

"There are many things we can try for that too, but again, for now I want you to try and use the Acceptance Method. It means that when the bouts of anxiety come on, just sit still and let it be, don't stress out, worry or try to get a hold of yourself—simply let it pass through your body and then get on with your day."

"Really, to do nothing is the best cure?" I was confused.

"Yes, part of the Acceptance Method that we teach here is to just let it be. Let it do whatever it wants to you and if you just accept that it's there and get on with life, do what you normally do and you'll see that it will soon subside. That's how to 'rewire' your brain and eventually you'll start to feel better again."

I came out of the first session confused—I thought she was going to give me some kind of medication to sort out those negative thoughts and stop my body from palpitating when the panic got worse, but instead, she told me the best form of treatment was to allow them to be while you get on with your day to day tasks until they start to fade away. I wasn't sure if they would, but I was determined to try.

Chapter 27

Finally Some Justice!

After another restless night, mustering up whatever strength I could, I jumped out of bed and got ready to return to school. I was desperate to get back to some sort of normality. Dad was already awake; he promised to walk me to school. He called and made an appointment with the Principal to help me explain everything about Mr Phillips.

As Dad and I approached the school gates, I saw a marked white police car parked in front, beside the entrance with its single blue lights still flashing silently. *Something serious must be happening. I wonder what it is?*

We arrived at the school and reported to the reception. I came in like most students in the school building in smart clothes, and my bag filled with my books, my planner and equipment—I didn't have any prepared mixed cookie dough ready to bake in Miss Alford's cooking studio.

"We've got a meeting at 8:50 with the Principal," I told the Receptionist, Mrs Banks.

"I know you have, my dear," she replied, "but I don't think that meeting will happen this morning, to be honest. The Principal is dealing with something very serious. I've had to cancel all of his meetings for this morning and re-schedule them."

"But this is serious too, Miss, that's why my Dad is here," I said, as my mind started to wonder what he was dealing with.

"I know, darling," she repeated, this time whispering, "it's the police, they're inside his office now speaking with him." My eyes lit up and I stood upright having bent over to speak to Mrs Banks.

"What? What for?" I asked.

"I don't know much, love, and I really can't discuss it to be honest," she replied, "but if you wait here until he's done, I'll see if he can see you quickly." That was the last bit I heard. Mrs Banks said some other stuff too, but very soon after she said "police," I stopped paying attention. I wanted to see what was going on. The police must have looked into everything I told them and their investigations must have led back to Mr Phillips. *Finally, some progress.* At last, maybe he'll get payback for all the dodgy dealings he was doing with his big thug of a side-kick Tooth Fairy Syed and his goons.

They were in the Principal's office right behind me. I looked in through the glass panes, but couldn't see anything. I wanted to go near the door so I could hear their conversation, but I knew I couldn't do that without someone noticing. The excitement and anticipation was too much—I had to see what was happening so I left Dad in the Reception area and slowly walked outside and sneaked behind the school to where the staff car park was. Just there, between the car park and the Year 11 playground, in the alleyway was the window to the Headteacher's office. I crouched down behind a few parked cars and past the Headteacher's PA's office. With my back to the wall underneath the window, which was slightly ajar, I turned my head to the left so that my right ear was directly underneath the open window. It was too late; I got there too late—they were all standing up and ready to leave.

"You'll have to come with us to the station," said a familiar female voice, "you've been read your rights and we'll have to cuff you since you pose a significant risk of absconding. We recommend that you get yourself some legal representation—expect a lengthy interview and questioning," concluded the familiar voice abruptly. I looked up to take a peek and saw Mr Phillips with his hands cuffed behind him as he was led out by two uniformed police officers. Another plain-clothed police officer followed; it was DCI Huntley. She did promise to look into everything I told her. What I told her probably sounded more like the script to a movie with all the juicy details about corrupt teachers and a wide network of criminals and thugs. Except it wasn't a script for a movie—it was only my surreal life and I was glad another chapter of it was slowly closing and coming to an end.

I looked to my left and saw our Principal, Mr Faulkner. With his eyes looking downward and his head lifted forward, using the thumb and index finger of his right hand, he rubbed the inner corners of his eyes underneath his glasses. He shook his head continuously as the police officers walked Mr Phillips out of the school in plain sight of all of the students and staff who were slowly arriving through the front entrance. It must have been embarrassing for him; I couldn't see his face to see if I could notice any signs of regret. I suspected he'd be defiant; he was arrogant like that. They marched him into the police car and drove off.

I let out a deep sigh of relief and closed my eyes. I imagined myself on a cloudless spring day standing barefoot on finely cut soft grass. The sky was blue and the temperature was so perfect I didn't even notice the weather. I looked around to admire the delicate blooming flowers that were all around me. I felt the warm sun rising inside my chest and reaching my throat. I pressed my lips to prevent the giggles that were steadily emerging from my mouth; not evil laughter at seeing the misfortune of someone else, but happy giggles coming from the pit of my belly. After a few seconds, my chest was shaking and I had to hold my mouth to stop the loud laughter from escaping. For a few minutes, that's all I did; with my back against the outside wall of the Principal's office and my body crouched down, I laughed hysterically. It tickled me to death that finally Mr Phillips was going to get the justice he deserved, and hopefully Syed and his goons too!

By the time I opened my eyes, the muscles of my cheekbones were hurting and the steady streams of warm tears were splattered across my face. All of a sudden, I remembered we had to meet the Principal, so I quickly ran back inside and sat next to Dad. A few seconds later, Mr Faulkner came out and invited us into his office.

"The police explained everything to me, Riya," he said, "I can only say that I'm really sorry for what you've had to go through and I have also heard from Stacy—she has confirmed my suspicions that you were set up," he continued in his usual formal tone.

"Does that mean I can have my old position back?" I looked at him with my jaw wide open.

"As far as I'm concerned, you can have your badge back and continue as you did." He slid my Prefect badge towards me.

I let out a deep sigh of relief.

"I'm glad it's all sorted and you can put all of this behind you!" said Dad, looking into my eyes.

"Just one more thing Riya," said Mr Faulkner, "it seems you've inspired some of our youngsters with your entrepreneurial skills."

"I have?" I asked, looking back at Dad, puzzled.

"Yes, you have and it's something I'd like you to take a lead on at this school."

"What do you have in mind, Sir?"

"I want to place you in charge of the Young Entrepreneurs Club, I want you to advise and mentor our eager youngsters, and yes," he added with a smile, "you can continue to sell your lovely baked cookies that I've heard so much about."

Chapter 28

Healing and Faith

The weather was a bit puzzling—it couldn't decide if it was going to be completely hot or completely cold and windy. The warmth of the unusual May sunshine that afternoon together with the small flurries of wind made the final day of school before we broke up for the summer half-term holidays feel very peculiar. I strategically arrived early to the whole school end of half term assembly so I could be the first person in the front row—that way I'd be the first to be dismissed. As I ran out of the main hall, I forced myself to stop in the empty forecourt of the school to absorb the warm winds while the rays of sunlight made me squint, a moment of peace, a moment of calm. But it didn't last long. Within a few seconds I heard the roar of the other students who were bursting with energy to quickly exit the school and enjoy the rest of the day. The usual early closures on the final day of each half term meant that we had even longer to stay out and mess around before our parents expected us home.

I walked home by myself—Anisa always stayed at home on the last day of school before a holiday with one excuse or another. I thought about the chaos of the early part of the school year, with the return of Mum's cancer and my desperate attempt to make money to pay for private medical care. A whole school year had almost passed, so quickly. It seemed like such a long time ago. Even the mayhem of Mr Phillips, Tooth Fairy Syed and the whole nightmare of being kidnapped by their thugs seemed like another lifetime ago, but really only a few months had passed. I guess that's how we humans cope with stuff, by allowing ourselves to forget things.

Mr Phillips was sent to jail following a court case, which the newspapers made a massive deal out of, and rightfully so! Who would have known Mr Phillips, who came from a privileged background and was a talented and hardworking teacher by day, but by night, was deeply involved in the criminal underworld? It didn't help that he tried to bring his daytime and nighttime passions together to profit even more. Tooth Fairy Syed and a load of boys belonging to his gang were also rounded up by the police after Mr Phillips' embarrassing arrest. No doubt Mr Phillips told them about everyone who was involved with him; he didn't seem like the "loyalty amongst criminals" type. I don't know what happened to Syed's gang or how many got caught, but Dad did say some of the slightly older ones ended up in the young offenders' prison where he worked. For now, things were quiet in our neighbourhood.

I saw Stacy on the day the police asked me to come into court to give evidence against Mr Phillips. Stacy also testified and told the court everything. Thankfully, the police didn't take any action against her because she helped them with their investigations and told them how she was threatened and forced to get involved.

Mum was slowly making a full recovery and so I didn't have those bitter feelings hanging around me like a shadow of death. She no longer needed regular treatment and was almost back to normal except that she shaved off all of her hair to help it grow back evenly. She was a lot happier and looked healthy—she was slowly going back to her normal weight. She was active again; doing the school runs and the shopping again by herself. Mum hated relying on people to get stuff done; being able to do things again by herself must have been like the return of an old friend. Her appetite also returned, as did the rosiness in her dimple-layered cheeks.

I continued my counselling sessions to help treat my PTSD, which I always found difficult and exhausting, but I was glad that I could open up more about my fears and anxieties, as well as that voice that still sometimes taunted me. I practised the things Amanda taught me including some mindfulness and breathing techniques to help me cope when the bouts of anxiety felt crippling. She also advised me to start some type of regular exercise to keep my mind and body active.

"I'm advising that you visit your GP, Riya, just to get some sleeping pills in order to reset your body clock," she said, "please don't worry about anything. A lot has changed over the last decade about how we view mental health in young people."

"Of course," I agreed.

"How have you been feeling since starting the sessions?" she asked, "At least I can see you're not reluctant to continue getting support."

"I have been feeling a lot better," I replied, "I know I still need it—the sessions are definitely helping."

"That's really good to hear," she smiled, "I can see it's helping—you can talk about things and open up easily, without breaking down. The fact that you can talk about your challenging experiences without panic and anxiety setting in and overwhelming you, is definitely a sign that you are better managing your symptoms."

"Yes, I do feel more in control of my thoughts and emotions," I nodded, "and I definitely feel more confident when a bout of anxiety comes on, I feel I can deal with it much better."

"That's really great, Riya," she replied, "we are making progress, but I do think a few more sessions and you will be where I want you to be. I think you could benefit from some more talking therapy in the long term since our sessions will end in a few weeks. Your GP surgery will sort that out for you. I'll send them an email now."

I was lost in thought as I walked home. I thought about everything that happened over the last few months, but it didn't upset me anymore and I definitely had a better grip each time I felt slightly anxious. I was happy with my progress; I never thought I'd be able to get a grip of how I'd been feeling. I looked up at the clear sky and let the rays of the sun stroke my face. I breathed in and closed my eyes for a few seconds. When I opened them, I saw Nadim walking towards me.

"Hi Riya," he said, his voice warm and calming.

"Hi there, Nadim," I replied, trying not to trip up on my words like I usually did when I spoke to him.

"It's great that you're back at school," he said, "I knew everything would work out in the end."

"Thank God," I replied.

"You look well by the way... I mean, like your face is glowing," he smiled, looking a bit embarrassed.

"I've had a good few days, that's all."

"That's brilliant. What have you been up to?" he asked.

I looked into his eyes and pressed my lips against each other. I didn't want to tell him, but for some reason, I felt I could. I took a deep breath before explaining to him the difficulties I was having after being diagnosed with PTSD. I even told him about the counselling sessions.

"Hopefully you won't judge me or look at me any different," I sighed.

"What? Don't be silly, Riya," he said, "it's really good to hear that the counselling sessions are helping." He then paused and looked away. "I had a course of counselling sessions a couple of years ago myself," he revealed.

"What? Really?" I asked. My eyes lit up. "How come, if you don't mind me asking?"

"I had a lot going on that year—long story, trust me." I looked up, his eyes were unfocused and searching behind me. "Things started to get on top and then something happened in school so my Head of Year referred me for some counselling. I was really against it at first, but then I realised that I needed the help."

"I'm glad it helped," I told him.

"Yeah, it helped me to look at things differently and get a better perspective on life," he explained, "the most important thing it taught me was to stop living inside my head, start living in the real world and take each day as it comes."

"That's so important. Sometimes events or experiences can overwhelm us. It does help to speak to a fresh set of ears without holding back, especially someone who knows how to help you like a counsellor."

"What about you, do you feel it's helping?" he asked.

"Yes, it is. I definitely feel much better and I feel I've got a better handle on my symptoms which were making me feel so horrible."

"I'm glad to hear it. Just continue with the sessions and stay the course, you won't regret it."

"Sure," I agreed, nodding.

"Anyway, I've got to go, see you around."

I watched Nadim walk off into the distance. I'm glad I spoke to him. I was surprised I was able to open up to him the way I did. That must be what my counsellor was referring to—being able to speak about my difficulties without breaking down or getting emotional. It definitely felt like I had reached another milestone by being able to open up to Nadim. My mind felt decluttered and my heart felt lighter.

Over the next few weeks, I regularly went to Regent's Lake Mosque with Anisa, especially on Friday afternoons to see how they observed the *jummah* prayers. I was a bit nervous on my first visit, but Anisa tried to keep me relaxed. We always got there quite early before it started filling up really quickly.

"Are you sure my clothes are alright?" I asked, looking down at my flared trousers and loose nylon shirt.

"Of course they are, babe," she replied, "you never wear tight or revealing clothes anyway. Here, wrap this loosely around your head, you don't have to pin it."

Anisa handed me a light blue scarf to cover my hair with. I placed it over my head to make sure that my hair wasn't showing before following Anisa to the women's prayer area. I listened to the Imam deliver the sermon in English and then sat behind the ladies as they offered the Friday prayer in congregation. When the prayer was over, I observed how the women embraced each other and greeted one another. I noticed how they spoke to each other mostly in English, but sometimes effortlessly changed to Urdu, Bengali and Arabic depending on what their native tongue was. Some of the "sisters" as Anisa called them stood around the coffee and cake stall just outside the prayer hall, sipping their drinks and sharing cakes with one another. Anisa dragged me everywhere she went and introduced me to all her mosque friends. There were so many of them; some from her old primary school, some from her Saturday Qur'an class, and a few from her block. They were all very happy to meet me and made me feel really welcome. There was definitely a strong sense of sisterhood.

I decided to look into Islam even more by reading more books from my library and reading articles online. I watched a few YouTube videos too made by Muslims from all over the world—I learned so much from men and women who spoke about Islam in a simple and easy to understand manner. I learned about the importance of charity, respecting your elders, being grateful to God and most importantly being true to yourself. I knew what I had to do, but the more I learned about Islam, it grew on me and made me even more certain of the decision I had made, but I kept putting it off.

After a while, I stopped delaying it. Islam really had made an impression on me so after a lot of "soul searching," I decided to accept Islam as my new faith and way of life. I told Anisa straight away, and she arranged for me to meet the Imam of Regent's Lake Mosque the very next day.

Even as I walked into the mosque that evening, I felt different; I felt tranquillity, peace. I heard the *azaan* for the *Magrib* (sunset) prayers, which sounded strange but soothing just like the Qur'an recitation that I was still listening to every night. It was a busy mosque, especially during prayer times—people were rushing about trying to get ready for prayer, the bookshop at the front of the mosque was closing its shutters and I saw young mums kneel down to take their children's shoes off before entering the prayer hall.

After the prayer, Anisa and I walked into the Imam's office, which was just outside the main prayer hall. I was shaking, my hands were trembling, I couldn't even speak. Nobody else was there; it was just me, Anisa and the Imam—that's how I wanted it. I wasn't ready to announce my new faith to the entire world; I still had no idea how Mum and Dad would react.

Anisa held my hand the whole time as the Imam explained to me what I was about to say and told me to repeat the testimony of faith after him. I repeated it in Arabic first and then in English.

"Congratulations, sister Riya," he smiled, "welcome to the family."

I heard Anisa's repeated chants of "*mashallah*" before embracing me.

"The next stage is for you to learn about your new faith, Riya," explained the Imam, "we have a wonderful New Muslim course starting in a few weeks. I hope you will join us."

"Of course," I replied, "I mean *inshallah*."

I had a quick wash and made *wudu* in the newly refurbished ladies' *wudu* and shower area. My hands were still trembling as I blow-dried my hair and wrapped a white floral patterned *hijab* loosely around my head, which Anisa pinned down for me. I swallowed hard and looked at myself in the mirror.

"This is you, girl," she smiled, "everyone needs to get used to it. It'll be fine *inshallah*." I looked up at her and took a deep breath before making my way home.

I knew I had to tell Mum and Dad before they started to notice changes in my behaviour. The most obvious thing they would definitely notice was my headscarf, which I planned to wear properly after I told them. Even if I secretly prayed in my room, I'm sure they'd eventually notice. So I didn't really have a choice, I had to tell them quite soon. I thought about what I would say, how I would say it and when the best time would be. I rehearsed it in my head so many times, but I was sure it would come out all muddled up—that's what usually happened when I had to speak under pressure. I decided I was going to tell them the following day—it was one of the most difficult things I had to do in my entire life!

I walked into the living room with my green prayer mat in one hand and my prayer beads in the other and sat on the single sofa beside Mum and Dad. Dad glared at me with his mouth wide open and Mum froze. I got up and kissed both of them, held their hands and kneeled down in front of them.

I felt my eyes filling up with tears as I looked at them both. "I love you two very much," I said, "and now I've made an important decision I hope you'll respect."

Dad's face turned dark red. "I had a suspicion," he said, "how? I mean why Riya? I can't do this, not now," he snapped. Dad stormed out of the living room. Warm tears rolled down my cheeks as I looked at Mum's face. I didn't know what to think or how to feel. A few seconds later I heard the door slam shut. Mum darted around and took a deep breath. Her face was expressionless. She opened and closed her mouth several times before being able to form words.

"Are you sure, Riya?" she finally asked, "Are you sure this is what you want? I had no idea."

"Of course, Mum, this is the life I've chosen for myself." I wiped my tears, stood up gazing at her face, searching for approval. "Why did Dad react like that?"

"It must be all the stuff in the newspapers and media," she replied, "it's difficult not to let that stuff in."

"But how come you're not like that, Mum—judgemental, I mean?"

"It's because I've had real-life experience and interactions with Muslim colleagues remember? That's what I use to make my judgements," she continued. "I'll talk to your dad—he's just had a lot on lately."

I hoped and prayed that Dad would eventually come around to the idea; I knew I needed to give him some time, so I just let him be. *It was still early days,* I thought to myself.

Dad ignored me for the next few days. He wouldn't even look at me. When I tried to make polite conversation with him, he would reply coldly and walk off. I didn't want to force him to speak about my new faith. He obviously still hadn't come to terms with it so I gave him time and space hoping he would approach me to talk about it when he was ready.

I still baked cookies with Mum's help, not because we needed the money so desperately anymore, but because I liked it. I enjoyed the independence of making my own money and helping out around the house. Thanks to Nadim's advice, I managed to set up a website, which was fully functional—it got a lot of traffic, but it still looked a bit plain even though we sold five different types of cookies! Anisa was always there to help. My next step was to try to scale up somehow—I didn't know how exactly, maybe a small stall somewhere. I had some dreams and plans in my head, but nothing urgent; it could wait.

Over the summer half-term break, I had to get ready to attend the Young Entrepreneur Awards in central London. Someone nominated me after hearing about my small online cookie business. I had a suspicion it was

Nadim, but I couldn't be sure. I got the invitation and they told me I'd have to prepare a short presentation about my challenges and current progress. I'm looking forward to the event, but not the presentation part. I hope I don't forget to take free samples for everyone!

The week off wasn't long at all, I knew it was going to pass very quickly. I had so much to do and final A-Level exams to sit. Plus, Ramadan was around the corner. I wondered how my body was going to adjust to not eating and drinking for all those hours, but I was looking forward to the new experience.

The sun went down as I stood on our small box-like balcony, absorbing the remaining warmth that was still present in the air. I felt it hug me and embrace me like a distant friend. I looked to my left, realising for the first time that I could actually just about see Nadim's tower block from here. I tried not to look back at all the things that happened over the past few months and weeks. I tried to look ahead, look forward to whatever the future held. Whatever came my way, I was sure, in the end, everything would turn out just fine.

Glossary of Arabic Terms

- [ ] Allah – The Arabic name for God

- [ ] Alhamdulillah – Praise be to Allah

- [ ] Azaan – The Muslim call to prayer

- [ ] Hijab – Islamic head scarf for women

- [ ] Isha – The night prayer

- [ ] Inshallah – God willing

- [ ] Jummah – Friday Prayers

- [ ] Magrib – Sunset prayers

- [ ] Mashallah – Praise be to Allah

- [ ] Qur'an – Muslim Holy Book

- [ ] Ramadaan – Muslim holy month

- [ ] Shahadah – Testimony of faith

- [ ] Wudu – Ablution